Valentius: A Werewolf Story

Valentius: A Werewolf Story
by
Arundell Overman

ISBN (9798353236689)

Table of contents:

Valentius: A Werewolf Story

The Trial

Hello dear reader, please allow me to introduce myself, my name is Valentius, and I would like to tell you the story of how I became a werewolf, and some of my adventures. I have lived a long time, and I have had a great many adventures, to write them all would take a lot of books. So, at this time, I will only tell a small part of my story, and perhaps if I live long enough, I will write more. The current date is 1887, I am 237 years old, and perhaps appear to be 40 or 50. You don't have to believe me of course, take this book as a work of fiction, of entertainment. I was born in 1650 in France.

When I was 19 years old, I came under the service of the King of France, as a court Alchemist. You see, the king at that time thought himself to be a student of the occult arts, of alchemy, of astrology, and such things, and he liked to surround himself with the sort of people who could indulge his interests. I was recommended for the post of court alchemist rather early in life, as my master, the old alchemist I had been an apprentice of, died suddenly, and I was left with partial training and a room full of alchemy books with which to carry on.

Fortunately for me, being my masters only student and the one who knew how to read his books, I was brought to live in the palace of the king, and given a room in one of the towers where I was told to read the books, and prepare to be an alchemist in the employ of the king, a post I much appreciated and treasured as anyone close to the king was guaranteed good meals and safe lodgings. So, there I was in my wizard's tower reading my books when I heard a knock on the door.

A thin man in his 30s with straggly black hair and a lazy eye appeared at my door. He announced himself as Nicolas and stated that he had been appointed to the post of court astrologer, and he had heard that I was a keeper of many strange books. He confided in me that him and I were the "wizards" of the court and said that maybe we could learn a few things from each other. Having no friends and being in a strange city, I was glad for the chance to talk to someone.

Nicholas and I began to look over the piles of books my master had left me and I was picking them up and talking a little about each one saying such things as "this one is for calcination, this one is on the philosophers stone, this one is said to be a rare treatise on fairies and gnomes, these are for finding treasure, this one is for conjuring spirits such as angels and demons, etc." Nicolas seemed particularly interested in a book with the names of demons in it. He picked one of those books up and began to look through it.

At that moment there was again, a knock on the door. A steward of the king was there and stated that the king required his "wizards" to accompany him on a short journey and they were needed immediately. So, Nicholas and I went with him to the throne room. There the king was waiting. The king was old and senile at this point, he had no battles to fight, no threats to his kingdom, and he was lost in his own outrageous wealth and grandeur. He sat on a throne looking bored and beside him, in great contrast to his age, was a beautiful and young queen. The Queen looked Nicholas and I up and down as if assessing us and finding nothing of interest, looked away.

"As the king, my presence is occasionally required during the trials of some evil people, witches and werewolves." the king said. "It is merely a formality, as I am not making any decision or involved in the case, but the people like to see that their king knows when justice is carried out." He paused for a moment and then stated that, "I am told that the guilty are to be executed, as the evidence against them is strong." "Come," he said to us, I want you to go with me, and Nicholas, please continue with the explanation of the sign of Pisces and the planet Jupiter as yesterday while we travel."

So, we got in the kings coach, and the king began asking Nicholas about the influence of the planets upon the lives of royals, and his birth chart. Nicholas really seemed to bloom then, taking on an almost different personality, very soft and eloquent, he charmed the king like a woman would, with flattery, telling him how his chart made him so awesome, and the poor old fool ate it up.

Soon we arrived at the courthouse, an ominous and threatening building. The king, Nicholas and I, and the king's attendants were led up to a balcony to observe the proceedings. A judge and jury came in and sat on a raised dais, and then the prisoners were brought forward in chains, a man, a woman, and a girl of perhaps 14 or 15 years old.

The evidence against them was then presented. A woman neighbor had come over to their house to borrow a pinch of salt and seen a book lying open on the table. It had strange symbols in it, and she suspected witchcraft and reported them to the authorities. The house had been searched and the book was found. It was presented as evidence. Portions of the book were read during the trial, which included a love spell calling upon the names of the demons Asmodeus and Lilith. This alone was enough to convict them, but the judge also stated that those familiar with the case had read other portions of the book which included such awful details as a ritual to conjure the dead, and even a spell to become a werewolf.

The king was bored by all of this, thinking only of himself, he continued to press Nicholas for information about his astrological chart, and I strained to hear the details of the trial. What was that about a werewolf book? The judge ordered the couple to be burned at the stake, and since there was no evidence to convict the daughter, she was sent to a convent. Suddenly an idea sprang to my mind, what was in the book? Was there really a spell to become a werewolf? What could such a thing be like?

"Valentius, have you ever had your birth chart done?" Nicholas asked me. "Huh?" I had been ignoring Nicholas and the king to watch the trial. Nicholas repeated the question and then asked me if I was enjoying the trial. He seemed amused by it all. The man and his wife were then led away in tears to be executed swearing that their spirits would get revenge on the neighbor who turned them in to the Inquisition. I shuddered to think of their fate. "Are you enjoying the trial?" Nicholas asked me again. "The witches' book," I murmured "I would like to see it." Nicholas turned to the king and asked him if we may see the witch's book. The king then ordered the book to be brought to my alchemy library, the trial was over, and we returned to the king's palace.

Studying the book

The next day I began to read the book. I found that it was divided into three chapters. The first chapter claimed to be an instruction manual for becoming a werewolf, written by one Marcus, and dated at 1492. The second chapter gave a spell for conjuring demons, and the third was a method of summoning ghosts. At the end of all this was given a spell to cause love or to separate lovers, depending on how it was used. I have always believed that there were once more spells, or other parts to the book, but perhaps they had been lost. I must have read the book a thousand times and can now write it from memory. The following is the full text of the book...

The Witches Book

Marcus speaks

Hello, my name is Marcus, and I am here to give you the most precious treasure in the world, the way to become more than a man, the way to become a god among men, a werewolf. I write these words in the year 1492 to my son and descendants, who, should they not be born a natural werewolf, they will be able to use the formula I have learned from my master, the great grandmother of the werewolves, she whose name must never be spoken, for she is able to travel through the veil, and she can hear all from her mountain cave where she lies sleeping.

I give you, my son, and indeed to anyone who is bold enough to carry out this work should they find this book, for who can know where a book will travel? I give you this precious power, a power with which wherever you go, you shall fear no man. And you will never get sick, and you will live to an unnatural age. You need not even fear the beasts of the forest, and can live in a cave if you wish, such is your freedom.

First you must know that if you follow these steps, once you change, there is no turning back. What you will become is between this world and the other world, the world of heaven and hell, the world of the dead, angels, demons, and other creatures. The longer you live, the more powerful you will become, the more a part of the other side, the other world. Yet in some way you must retain a part of this world, until you die, or cross over to the dream world and take your body with you, as some of us are said to be able to do. There are others beyond me, but I need not tell you of the ancient ones here, it is enough that you know of my existence, and that I had a master once, even though I will not speak her name because it is too dangerous for you. If some reader by chance were to speak her name, she might come through the veil and kill them in an instant, for she is in the beyond now, my master.

So let me tell you the way I know, it is like the ancient way, with a few things I added to it to make it easier and safer, and so that it can be done alone. In ancient times, werewolves were always made by a group of people initiating a new person into the group through frightening rituals which could scare a person to death. My method is a bit different, more modern, but I can tell you that it works, because I saw four of my students' become werewolves before my eyes. 3 of them still roam in this world, and one has died tragically. That is a long story, but I am writing to you with a purpose my son, so we shall skip the details of my life and my loves and explain the method by which you may attain this precious gift of power.

First, you must conjure and bind 5 demons and 7 ghosts, using the methods given in the second and third books. The demons may be taken from the books of magic, and they can be any 5 demons which you have personally met. The 5 demons which I have written of in this book are spirits which I personally met, and I used them to help me transform, you may conjure these demons, or others, any 5 will do. The sigils of the ghosts shown here are the 7 ghosts which I conjured. You must find your own ghosts, mine are with me. The 7 ghosts must also be people whom you have known in your life. If you do not know 7 people who have died, you must conjure the ghosts of those who have been hanged or died tragically, and this is more difficult, for these ghosts are restless and dangerous.

Then, you must go alone and build a house in the woods which you can live in for several months as you begin the first transformation. Once you have done it, the power is yours for life. So go alone to your house in the woods, where no one knows where you are, and tell no one where you are going, you will stay in that place until you are changed for the first time and then have the power for the rest of your life.

Remember that you must observe every detail, or you could bring upon yourself either failure or misfortune. For the whole time that you enter the woods you must abstain from the hidden offices, do not give into your lusts, you must be full of desire. Also, you must moderate your diet so that you only eat once every 12 hours, and you must fast once a week. Wait until your stomach rumbles like thunder to eat, and never eat too much, always thinking of moderation, and the great enterprise upon which you have set yourself. You must drink no wine and eat no sweets during this time, and you must not give in to idle thoughts of the past and future, but only observe the moon, and the creatures of the forest as you gather and prepare the herbs and the oil of transformation which has been handed down to us by the ancient ones.

You will gather the 4 herbs, Wormwood, Henbane, Belladonna, and Poppy. Grind all of this to a powder and mix it within a large amount of fat made from that of a pig. Heat the fat and herbs gently, when this cools, spread it all over your naked body while wearing the skin of a wolf tied tightly to you.

Perform this experiment standing inside the magic circle which has the sigils of the 5 demons and the 7 ghosts written upon it as shown in this book. You will follow the instructions in the second and third parts to properly make the magic circle and summon the 5 demons and 7 ghosts. They will be bound to you, and give you power when the moment of change comes. You must call the names of the 5 demons and 7 ghosts before you put on the skin. They will see what you are doing and guide you and help you to accomplish the great work of the transformation.

This is where things get difficult because it may happen at any time then due to a variety of conditions. You will have to go very slowly at first because the power of the herbs is so strong that you must begin with them very diluted so that you can understand what happens when the power comes. At first you may only feel a bit strange. Then you will probably begin to see things, bright colors, or shapes of things changing to look like snowflakes. Don't worry about all that and just wait till it is over and then try again 3 days later.

You might have to stay out in your cabin in the woods for two or three months, maybe even six, but sooner or later, you will get it right, you will feel a wolf inside you, the ghost of the one whose skin you are wearing, it will come to you and become one with you, and then you will have the power inside you of generations of wolves, over thousands of years, and you will see things you can never truly explain about everything, and the birth of the sun and other stars, and all of it. And then you will change, and I myself will appear to you, and you will leave your human form behind and run through the forest.

The Demons

In the Name of Murmur, Egyn, Paymon, Asmodeus, and Lilith, I conjure this book to be profitable to those who shall possess it. By the signature of the demons bound within the book, I command that the contract be fulfilled when the book be opened, and the devils of hell be summoned forth to fulfill the requisites of their pact.

Murmur rules over the legions of the dead and can bring any soul to stand before the magician, Egyn teaches music and magical arts such as how to cause spirits to be bound to books, Paymon can crush the enemies of the magician and give familiar spirits as servants, Asmodeus, is the teacher or instructor in strategy and the art of accomplishment, and Lilith, is the lustful one.

To conjure the demons, enter the magic circle with the book, and a wand made of cherry tree wood upon which are written, carved, or burned, the names of the 5 demons of the book. Take with you incense made from dried and powdered cherries. Face the direction which the demon is to appear, which will be one of the points of the magic circle diagram, and then say.

"Oh, thou demon from the pit of hell, I call you in the name of the ever living and infinite power which has no name, the power which animates your very souls and causes the stars to shine and the planets to move through the heavens. Come unto me now and write your seals and characters in my book, swearing obedience unto me as I swear obedience to you. Receive this incense as an offering in the name of Satan, the one who rules all rebel spirits in Hell, and make a contract and a pact with me to give me the secrets of the universe, wealth, treasures, the love of my desire, and whatever powers you can share with me as one who is to become as you are, eternal, and immortal."

You may use the sigil of the demon found in the books of magic, or you may get the spirit to show you a sigil. The sigils of the demons are like keys to open the doors of power within the magic circle, and your soul. These spirits can be conjured for many purposes, but their purpose here is to give power to the great transformation into a werewolf.

Here follows the sigils of the 5 demons:

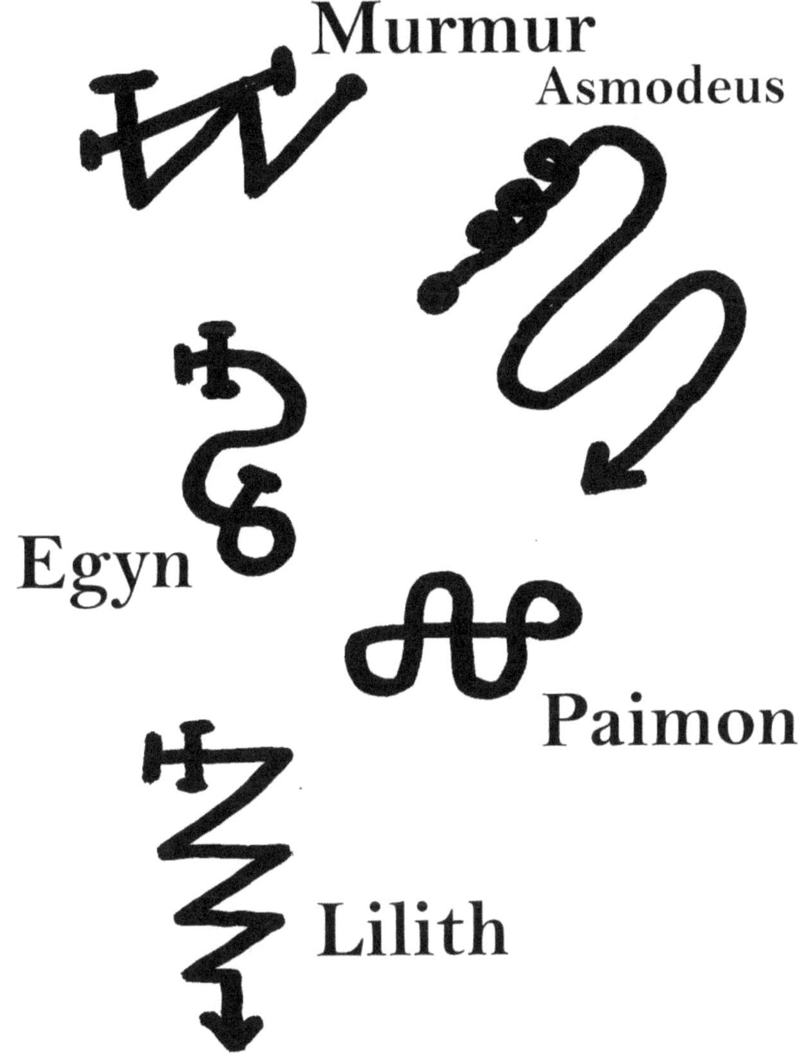

Place the sigils of the 5 demons in the inner ring of the magic circle, at the points of the pentagram.

Here follows the form of the magic circle:

Conjuring the dead

First you must know that to become a necromancer is no small thing, for when you enter the graveyard to do one experiment, you will attract the notice of every spirit who lives there, and some may follow you for the rest of your life. Yet it is necessary for the work of the werewolf, for it is in communication and connection to the dead that you will open the door between the worlds so that the spirit of the wolf within the skin may come to you.

A graveyard is a home for many spirits, and a realm into its own. To conjure any spirit which lies in the cemetery, you will go to the place when no one else is around, dig up the body and take the skull. Take the skull to a safe place where you can make the magic circle and conjure the spirit. Remember to use the wand made of cherry wood, and to burn incense made from dried cherries. When you are thus prepared, place the skull on the edge of the magic circle over its sigil, and standing within the circle, turn in the direction the spirit is to appear and say:

"I call you by the master of the graveyard, the one unto whom you owe obedience to make your residence here. Come unto me now and appear visibly so that I may speak with you and discuss matters as I see fit. I promise to satisfy you in the things which you once loved when living, by making offerings of those things unto you in return for service and knowledge of the doings of the other world. Come unto me now by the master of the graveyard, come unto me in the name of Charon, who guides the boat of the dead across the river Styx. I conjure you to fulfill my will in all things without any falsity."

Then you shall see the spirit of the one you have conjured appear and begin to speak with you. You must be courteous and receive them as you would a king, yet firm as one would address a subject. Remember that your exchange must be in the form of gifts and that they must fulfill your will in all things, both in action and the giving of hidden knowledge, of which they know an infinitude of things, yet not all, for this is kept by greater spirits than these. You will bring a gift of something to the spirit as you conjure it, something which it loved during its life, and in return it must give you a sigil or symbol by which it can be known and conjured. You will do this 7 times and carefully record the 7 sigils of the ghosts which will obey you. Remember to bathe twice a day and to abstain from all uncleanliness both of body and soul, for these are the traps with which spirits will drag you down into Hades with them.

Here follows the 7 sigils of the dead:

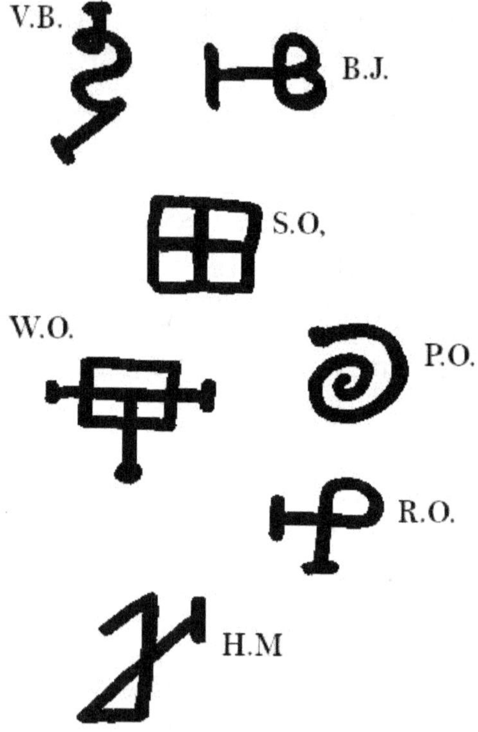

Place the sigils of the 7 ghosts in the outer ring of the magic circle.

To cause love by the power of the demons Lilith and Asmodeus.

First know that Asmodeus is the lord of lust and desire, and this has been proved since ancient times when he fell in love with the mortal woman Sarah, and that Lilith is the ancient mother of harlots. So together these demons can cause anything to happen in matters of love.

You will make two talismans, these are to be in the form of magic squares like the book Abramelin, with the names of Asmodeus and Lilith around the edges. Then you will make two dolls of paper or cloth and color one red and the other green. Lay the green doll onto the Asmodeus square, and the red doll onto the Lilith square. Let this sit for three days, no more no less. Then sew or tie the two dolls together with twine. Place the names of the lovers on the inside touching each other, and the names of the demons on the back. Wrap this with the talismans themselves and tie together once again. Offer incense to the spirits, wave the wand over the dolls, and say:

"Oh, thou demons Asmodeus and Lilith, I conjure you to come forth and make this spell work in the intended way as it has been created. Bring together x and y in love, until I untie the dolls let them be together. What the demons hath brough together, let no man be able to separate, for it is in union until the end of the age."

Then hide the dolls in a place where no one can find them. When it is desired to separate the lovers, find the dolls, and untie them.

Note, to separate a couple, perform the instructions in reverse by first tying them together, and then untying them and removing each doll some distance away from each other, but a good magician could figure this out, so I need speak no more of it. Begin this spell in the waxing moon, and to untie, begin with the waning moon...

End of the Witches Book

The room behind the bookcase

Studying the witches book left me with strange feelings. When reading it I often felt a strange sensation, as if something, or somethings were watching me read. Once I had read it once, I had no reason to read it again, but I did, over and over. I tried to imagine the life that the witches had, and the writer of the grimoire, the mysterious Marcus, did he really write the book in 1492? And what of the demons and spirits in the book? Why would someone attempt to conjure such things? I spent time thinking about what I had learned in church on the few occasions I had been inside one. Heaven, Hell, God, Jesus, and the angels, demons, and saints all spun through my head. One day Nicholas came to my room, he wanted to study the Alchemy books as usual, at this time he had read quite a few of them. "What did you learn from the witches book?" He asked. "Have you become a werewolf yet?" He looked at me and smiled slyly. I had the feeling that his morals were not as pure as mine and I said "no!" in a rather shocked tone. "Why not?" he asked casually and smiled.

I asked myself the same question then. Why not? What were these books to be used for if not to carry out the experiments in them? I looked around my room at the 500 or so books. I knew their content; they were concerned with every sort of supernatural mystery that men had pondered for the past 1,000 years. But I had never carried out the instructions in any of those books, only seen my master perform certain experiments which today might be classed in the science of chemistry. Distilling pure alcohol, mixing it with powdered herbs, and drawing out the essence of the herb by evaporating out the alcohol, leaving only the pure essence of the herb behind in the form of an oil. That I could do. My master had left me his equipment, glass bottles and tubes and a way to apply gentle heat to them through a small fire which a bellows increased the heat of when needed.

"Do you really believe a man could become a werewolf?" I asked Nicholas instead of answering his question. "I don't know," said Nicholas, I don't know if any of this is real, these books, angels, demons, spells... werewolves." "But what if it was?" "What would you do then?" "Would you do it, become that thing..." He trailed off and stared into space. "What would it be like?"

I wondered what it would be like, and imagined myself running through the forest, half beast, half man. "The book says that the one who wrote it did so in 1492," I told Nicholas. If that is so, and he gave the book to the witches in the past say 20 years, that would mean, say…" I stopped and calculated the date, it was currently the year 1670, "if the book was written in 1492, and given to the witches in 1660, that would mean that the writer would have to have been almost 200 years old at the time he gave it to them…"

"Is he still alive?" Nicholas asked me. "I don't know, the book doesn't say, I never thought of that" I replied. "Can I read the book?" Nicholas asked me. I felt myself tighten defensively. I did not want it to be out of my sight. Nicholas looked at me calmly, sensing my struggle. "Don't worry," he said, I will come here and read it, and copy it as I read so that I may have my own copy of the book to study. That seemed agreeable to me, and it felt good to have someone to talk to about the book, someone who knew its contents and would understand.

As the days went by and the seasons changed, over the course of a month, Nicholas came to my tower room and read the book and made a copy of it for himself. We talked about the book's contents often, and heaven and hell, and salvation. I found that I was the only one worried about such things. Nicholas seemed much more inclined to the darkness, and often expressed his desire to meet one of the demons written about in the book, or a ghost.

Spirits scared me, ghosts even more so than demons, I just felt a sense of dread and doom when I thought of them, yet cemeteries were peaceful for me to walk through.

Sometime during the fall Nicholas came by to visit me. "Valentius," he said, "I want to try a magical experiment from one of the books." "But these things are against the law…" I began. Yes, we have these books, and we shouldn't have some of them I suppose… the church doesn't like them, we get away with studying them because we are part of the court of the king." "Yes, exactly, and since we are part of the court of the king, shouldn't we use them, shouldn't we go about carrying these things out?" "But you are an astrologer," I began, "not a conjurer." "And I am an alchemist, or one in training." Your job is to predict the future for the royal house, and my job is to make the philosophers stone, or turn lead into gold, as they say the masters can do." "Yes, but all of these books are part of your master's library, all of them, shouldn't we be using all of the knowledge, even summoning demons and ghosts?" "What else were these books written for?"

He had me there, my master had died before I had completed my training. I had been brought to the palace of the king under the assumption that I would study my masters' books and someday be able to carry out the most high-level alchemical experiments known. But what of the other books, the ones with the spells and rituals, and conjurations to spirits? These were also in my master's collection. Nicholas was looking at me. "I guess you are right" I said slowly. "I want to summon a demon," said Nicholas. There it was, the first sin, the first great step away from what was normal, or known. "I want to try the werewolf spell" I said before I could stop myself. If Nicholas could speak of summoning demons, I suppose I could talk to him about becoming a werewolf.

"We must keep each other's secrets." Said Nicholas, "you know this." I nodded. "I need a place, we need a place, to try some of these things out," said Nicholas. He then said that where he was staying, on the other side of the palace, was too close to other people, and that he was afraid that if he drew a magic circle on the floor, he might get caught and that would lead to trouble. I looked around my room, it was high in a tower, and no one ever came up to it except Nicholas. Then I thought of the king's messenger who had come to my room, and a maid who brought me food sometimes.

We could not take any chances. What we really needed was a secret room. In one corner of my tower room, there was a sort of large closet. I got the idea that we might build a bookshelf that went from floor to ceiling and put it on hinges, and that it could work as a door which would make the closet hidden from view should anyone come to the room. The room was only about 9 feet by 9 feet in size, but that should be large enough to make a magic circle, and store supplies and such for magical experiments from the books.

So, Nicholas and I created a large bookshelf, and covered the entrance to the smaller room. Then we created a second bookshelf inside the secret room, and placed a couple of chairs in there, and began to study in earnest. Nicholas created the magic circle and made a wand for the invocation of the demons, and I began to gather the herbs required for transformation.

The Queen

Here is where my story takes a turn of great wickedness. I was led into this wickedness by a woman, of course. So, it was with Adam and Eve. Adam would have never eaten the apple on his own, he was lured into it by his wife, who was lured into it by Satan. Are not we all on the dark path not led into it by numberless legions of demons? Yet I Valentius, I swear to you that I have always been a man of Character. Or at least I wanted to be, I tried to be.

There I was, in my wizard's tower, and I received a visit from the queen. I was sitting at a table I had constructed, surrounded by books. There was a knock on my door, I yelled to come in, and a beautiful young woman entered. I was expecting Nicholas and was not properly dressed for company. The young woman introduced the queen herself who entered my room as I hastily put on a shirt. She turned to the young woman and said, "leave us." The young woman stood outside the room and the door closed, leaving me in the room with the Queen.

I was all sorts of scared, nervous because she was so beautiful. She looked at me calmly as if assessing her effect on me. I swallowed nervously waiting for her to speak. "It has come to my attention that you are a keeper of strange books." She stated this matter of fact and paused. "Yes, my lady." "Tell me about them." I picked up several books and began to speak about their contents. She listened for a little on each one and then asked me to continue to the next one. I explained that the books of which I were the keeper came from my master, Basil Valentine, and that my name Valentius was a variation of his. I told her that if I ever had a student that I was also to name him as such, for every teacher in our line must bear the name.

She was very interested in the books, and I, like a fool, felt important for telling her what I knew about them. She said that she could read and had learned as a little girl. She said her mother wanted her to learn to read and had taught her. We talked about book after book, for about an hour. I started to feel like I was very smart. I even found myself sneaking looks at her soft skin, and her beautiful dress. This was the closest I had ever been to such a beautiful woman. I thought to myself that it was a pity that she was married to such an old, feeble, and boring king, when she was only a few years older than me. I wished I was king and could make love to her. These thoughts were mixed with feelings of guilt at even having them.

"Its amazing that you are allowed to keep these books, because you are in the service of the king, his alchemist, and yet, these books would be burned by the church," she said after examining a particularly demonic book which contained instructions for making a pact with Beelzebub. I had never thought of this fact before. My master had always stated that Alchemy was a holy art, even if the church despised it. I wondered then why so many of the books he left me with contained instructions for summoning demons. Yes, there were angels in them as well, and even the dead and fairies, but most of the spirits given were clearly demonic. "I suppose the rules are different for us," the queen said looking at me in the eyes. "The royal court," she explained when I looked lost, "things are different for us." I felt that she was implying that I was a part of that royal court, and since I worked for the king, and lived in his palace, being considered one of his wizards along with Nicholas, I had to agree.

I suddenly felt more special than in my whole life, here was the queen saying that I was part of the royal court, special. I noticed her breasts then, and her deep, blood red dress. Was she charming me? I had a moment where I sort of felt confused. Who was this woman and what did she want from me?

"The king tells me that you have a book that was taken from some witches," the Queen stated softly. "Yes," I said eagerly, thinking that it was exciting to be in possession of another dangerous and banned book, this one with an even more frightening story behind it. I looked for it among the piles of books on my desk for a moment and then it hit me. The book was in the secret room. The only way to get it would be to open the door that was the bookcase and enter the secret room. Nicholas and I had taken to studying it in the secret room, as I had the book for 6 months by that time, and we thought that the king had forgotten it, as I am sure that he had, yet somehow he must have mentioned it to the Queen in a passing comment and she had learned of it and remembered it, noting the detail for later in her mind.

What now? The Queen was looking at me sweetly. I had to decide. I could not say I lost it, that would show me a very poor steward of the books it was my job to be reading and studying. Yet I could not go into the secret room to get it for that would reveal the existence of the room itself. Time seemed to pass slowly then as my mind frantically sought an answer. I did not know what to do or say. "Nicholas has the book," I lied. It was as if my body had suddenly said the words and I was unable to stop it. It seemed a better alternative than opening the door to the secret room to get the book. If I did that, the Queen might see the magic circle drawn on the floor of the room and realize that Nicholas and I had been preparing to do far more than read these old books or carry out operations of Alchemy.

"Is that so?" the queen said and leaned back slightly in her chair. It was a subtle movement, but I felt her draw away from me. It was agony for me to feel as if I lost her attention even for a moment when before we had been talking so enjoyably about the books. She stood up as if to leave and stated that our visit had come to an end for the time being. "Perhaps you could come back tomorrow, and I can get the book by then and you can take a look at it." I felt that I sounded desperate to get her attention and once again had conflicting emotions about why I had offered to get the book from Nicholas by the next day. I knew that I wanted her to like me and to return to talk to me and think that I was important. Yet at the same time I felt like a fool for even thinking these things. Who was I to her? Nothing, she was a queen. "That would be wonderful," she said with a smile. Suddenly I felt like she liked me again, and I blushed and felt like a fool all at once. She left the room.

After she was gone, I sat in my room with my heart beating in stunned silence. What had just happened? The book! I opened the door to the secret room and ran inside to get the book, bringing it out into the main room. I then imagined the Queen coming the next day to see the book. My heart swelled with pride. I sat the book on my table and thought about her dreamily.

Nicholas! Where was he? I had to find him and tell him about the Queens visit. I had to tell him to lie and say that he had the book, and that he had given it back to me in time for the Queens visit tomorrow. I decided to take no chances and go looking for him immediately. What time of the day was it? Still around noontime. Where might he be at this time? His room perhaps? I rushed out of my room and went to look for him.

Nicholas

I found Nicholas in his room. He smiled at me as he opened the door. He seemed to be in a light, easygoing mood. I was out of breath from running. "What's the hurry?" he asked me with a raise of his eyebrow. I looked around me. "Can I come in?" I asked. "Sure," he opened the door and led me into his room. He sat in a chair, and I paced as I spoke.

"I have had a visit from the Queen to my room today." Nicholas looked at me curiously. "And?" "I lied to her," I blurted out. I raised my hand and waved it excitedly and rolled my eyes. "She asked me about the book, and it was in the secret room and so I told her you were borrowing it." Then, as if to add further explanation I said, "I couldn't go into the secret room to get it, or she would know that we are trying to use the book." Nicholas nodded and looked thoughtful. "She just came up to your room and asked about the book?" "Why would she do that?"

"I don't know," I said. "She came to my room and asked about all of the books I keep, I don't know why, maybe she just thinks those sorts of things are interesting." Nicholas looked at me skeptically. "So, if she asks you about it, then tell her you had it, but you gave it back to me, and now I have it." "I have never spoken to the Queen, ever," Nicholas stated flatly. "She will not ask me about it. I have only seen her in the presence of the king, and no man will even dare to speak to her in the presence of the king for fear that it might be thought of as being improper." He looked at me and then stated, "It is strange that she came to your room, did she have anyone with her?" "No, well she had a girl with her that she made stand outside the room when we talked." I added then, "she is coming back tomorrow to see the book."

"Why?" asked Nicholas. "I don't know, curiosity perhaps." I told Nicholas then about what she had said about the fact that members of the royal court could look at these books and study them, even though they were banned by the church. "You didn't tell her what we're doing did you?" Nicholas asked me accusingly. "No!" I yelled at him, and then lowered my voice. "There is a difference between keeping these books, and studying them..." I trailed off "...for Alchemy" I finished, then said "Alchemy is a holy art." I didn't know who I was trying to convince.

"Members of the Royal court or not, we might be hanged if word got out that we are trying to use the witches' book to become werewolves," said Nicholas. He continued "I thought the king had forgotten about it, you know, he didn't seem to even be paying attention to the trial that day, he ordered the book to be brought to your chambers because he thought it was simply a curiosity." "I know," I said, he thinks that Alchemy and Astrology are Royal arts, like Music, and that they are far removed from the books used to call spirits and cast spells, but the truth is all of those sorts of books are the same, they all have magic in them." I looked off into space and then said, "It's all a sin, its all outside the church, it's all sorcery, even the books that have angels in them, its witchcraft."

"Yes, of course," said Nicholas coldly. "I am surprised that it has taken you this long to see it." "The Queen is right; we are allowed to do this because we are in the court of the king." "Don't ever let the word get out that you are doing anything other than the most holy of experiments from those books, or even you could face trial just like those witches." "It is one thing to have the books, and it is another to summon a demon or to become a werewolf." Suddenly Nicholas and I looked at each other, it was as if we both had the same thought at the same time. He spoke it aloud "that's why she wants to see the book." "No, it can't be," I protested. I could not imagine the Queen wanting to become a werewolf.

Nicholas looked at me angrily "You think she likes you don't you!" "No..." I didn't sound very convincing. I knew that to say the Queen had any thoughts of me whatsoever would be the height of foolishness, but at the same time I wanted it to be so. "Why else would she come to your room and talk about the books?" Nicholas demanded. I didn't know what to say, I felt like he was angry with me and that added to my confusion about the situation. "I don't know!" I yelled at him.

"You can't trust a woman," Nicholas began, "they are sneaky, always up to something, always with some hidden motive, always lying." I felt that surely this had to be an awful assessment of the Queen even though I had only spoken to her once. "Surely she wouldn't…" I began. "Oh, surely she would!" said Nicholas scornfully. "I am sure that tomorrow she will see the book and then that is all, she will leave my room and I will never talk to her again" I said. I found myself hoping this were not so. "What if she wants you to read the book to her?" Nicholas asked. "She can read," I said out, "Her mother taught her." "Is that what she told you?" "Yes."

"I didn't know any of this was going to happen!" I pointed out. Nicholas nodded, "Its true," he said quietly. "I think she wants the book for herself, its fortunate that I have made a copy of it." He turned to me then with a lot of intensity. "You can't tell her anything!" "I would never dare" I said. "You might think that now, but a woman that beautiful has her ways of getting what she wants." "She doesn't know anything," I said. "Ok, Ok," he calmed down a little then and I left his room and returned to my own in the tower.

The Queen Returns

I could barely sleep that night. In the morning at the same time the queen arrived with her attendant. Once again, she made her attendant stand outside the door and she came into my room. This time she casually sat down in a chair across from me and asked to see the book. I brought it out. It certainly did look mysterious. It was bound in a dark leather and looked as though it might be several hundred years old. It was written in an ink of unknown sort, possibly blood, and the skin it was bound in was also of an unknown kind, and I thought it might be that of a wolf, though of course there was no hair left on it.

The Queen stared at the book in awe for a moment. Then picked it up from the table and looked through it. She stopped for a moment to look at the magic circle design and the mysterious sigils of the demons and ghosts. She handed it back to me and then said, "now read it to me." I had no choice but to do as she commanded, after all, she was the Queen.

I read her the whole book from start to finish, it was not long, and the reading of it took me about an hour. She sat quietly through this whole time staring off into space. I could not tell what she was thinking. At the end of it all, she said while shaking her head, "what a curious book!" I did not know what to say. I waited for her to ask some question and wondered if she would be leaving soon and if I would ever see her again like this, where it was just the two of us. Then I thought that it did not really matter anyway, after all she was the Queen, what did I think, that I was falling in love with her or something?

I realized that she was looking directly at me then as if studying me. I felt very uncomfortable. I straitened my shoulders and tried to pretend I was important, after all, she had said I was a member of the royal court. I tried to feel that moment of vain self-importance again. "What is your name?" The Queen asked me. I snapped into the present moment. "Valentius." I replied, "my master was Basil Valentine," I said, as my master had taught me to say. It was almost like a part of my name, to say who my teacher was. It was as if I was referring to my father. And he had been like a father to me, for I was an orphan.

"Valentius, do you ever use these books to do any of the things within them?" "For instance, have you ever conjured an angel, demon, ghost, or a fairy, or have you ever turned lead into gold or made the philosophers stone, or cast a spell?" I did not know what to say, I had not done any of those things. I told her that I was only an alchemist in training when my master died, and that he had left me with all these books and I did not know how to use them and had not even read them all, that was my task, to read them, and become an alchemist. I told her that in the past year since I had come to the palace to live in the king's court, I had read 24 of the 500 books on Alchemy, which was a great task, since each of those books were 500 pages long. This may sound like a tall tale, but I assure you, many men wrote books of that size during those days.

"And when do you think that you will begin to carry out experiments in the service of the king, and what sort of experiments will they be?" She asked me. "Well, I have seen my master distill the essence of a rose from the petals many times before, and I believe that this will be the first experiment that I will attempt to carry out on my own," I explained. She seemed interested in this process and asked me to explain it. I showed her several glass bottles and tubes which could be used to purify alcohol. "It's like this," I said, first you get wine and put it in this bottle here, then you put this bottle over a real gentle flame, but you need to have this tube connected to it." What you are doing is trying to get the purest alcohol possible, because it has the power to cause the secret essence of the rose to separate from the flower and mix with the alcohol. Then, you heat it slowly, so that you cause the alcohol to fly out of it, like a bird, leaving the oil in this bottle, and its pure, and wonderful.

I opened one of the books and showed her some pictures. "I understand this book the best," I said, its basic alchemy. "Other alchemists can do more advanced things, such as purify metals and separate them, but I can't do any of that yet, and besides, it is very dangerous, and would require a lot more equipment than I have here with these glass tubes and bottles." Then I added "but I will do all of that when I am ready, I will have to aske the king for money to get some of the equipment, when I am ready, its dangerous, men have died from explosions of Alchemy work and that is often why people have said that it was the work of the devil." "You probably know the story of Faust, he sold his soul to the devil for his dark powers, and the devil taught him Alchemy, he was one of the first Alchemists, some say he died, others say that he is immortal."

"Really?" The Queen asked. She smiled at me and looked so beautiful then that I felt all sorts of confusing feelings again. She seemed to truly enjoy my company, or perhaps it was just that she liked to talk of strange things such as Alchemy and the devil. "And what do you think?" She asked me. "Did he die, this Faust, or did he use the power of Alchemy to become immortal?" "And did he sell his soul for this power, is that what you have to do?"

"I like to think he made it to immortality." I said hopefully. "And his soul?" she asked. "Ah, perhaps the devil gets that in the end I said, perhaps at the end of the world, Alchemists go to hell, they say Faust knew all of the pleasures of the world, had magical powers, and was loved by beautiful women."

"And what about werewolves," she said, "do they exist?" What about the book you have, the book of the witches, the one they died for, surely werewolves lose their souls and become children of darkness, children of Satan." She looked at me directly as if studying me and I had a strange feeling. Suddenly the conversation seemed very heavy. Deep inside I remembered the words of Nicholas. "Don't tell her anything!" I heard him say in my memory, "she wants the book for herself, you can't trust a woman, they are always lying,"

"Surely they do lose their souls to the devil, my Queen," I said. I thought that I had better play innocent, I could never admit that I might be tempted to give into such dark desires, such dark magic.

She simply smiled at me then and stood up to leave. "Thank you for reading the witches book to me and giving me an explanation of the books you have been trusted with," she said. I felt that she was very distant then, and that we were far apart, she a queen and I a subject, even if I was within the king's court. And that was as it should be, must be, no matter how beautiful she was. She said goodbye to me then and stated that perhaps she would come again to talk with me about the books. "Goodbye" I replied and then she was gone.

Necromancy

The next few days passed uneventfully. Then late one night there was a knock on my door and Nicholas came into my room with a burlap bag. He shocked me by dumping its contents out on my table and I could see that the bag contained 3 human skulls. "I have been busy!" Nicholas said with a smile. "What have you done?" I asked in a shocked tone. "Where did you get these?" "I dug them up!" Nicholas replied. I was stunned. Nicholas picked up one of them. "This is my aunt Bertha!" He exclaimed proudly. I gasped. Nicholas looked at me curiously. "Well, do you want to do this or not?" He asked me. "How else are we going to bind the spirits of the ghosts needed to become a werewolf?" My mouth hung open. I had not expected this. But Nicholas, you can't go around digging up bones like this, its wrong, and what if someone saw you, you would be executed, and now you have brought the skulls here, my God..."

"Its fine," said Nicholas, "no one saw me dig them up, they come from a graveyard where no one goes much anymore, and I filled the graves back in." He paused for a moment and then continued, "I had help, I hired some shady characters from the rough part of the city and paid them for their silence." I rolled my eyes; I did not know what to say. I supposed it was time to go all in, and really begin the experiment. "Ok, put them in the secret room," I told Nicholas. We opened the bookshelf door and went into the room, on the floor, Nicholas had painted the magic circle. He took the skulls and placed them around the edges, in the places where the sigils of the ghosts would go. "Now we have to conjure them and get the sigils." He spoke. I knew it was time, I looked around the room, were we ready? We entered the magic circle for the first time. Nicholas seemed to know what he was doing and held the Cherry wood wand. He lit some coals and set the powder from the dried cherries on it, the smell wafted through the room, then he began to conjure the spirits.

Presently the spirit of a rather fat woman with white hair appeared. She cursed Nicholas soundly for digging up her skull. I could hear her yelling at him but only make out some of the words. "How dare you desecrate my body in this manner Nicholas? You always were a dirty boy, and stupid. What would your mother say? You will go to hell for this boy!" Nicholas smiled and said, "My mother will know about this soon enough, and I wont care what she says, I can promise you that!" "What do you want from me?" The woman asked. "I want you to give me a sigil, a symbol that I can use to summon you." "And why should I do that?" The woman demanded angrily. "Because I will help you, get you something, do something for you, surely there is something you want?"

The woman seemed surprised by this, as if she had never considered making deals with the living. "What made you happy in life?" Nicholas asked her sweetly. I remembered him charming the king with his talk of Astrology.

"Well, I...I would like a good shot of whiskey," the woman said. "Ah that's good, that's good," said Nicholas, "I can get that for you, give me your signature, so I will have it when I call you again." "Give me the whiskey first!" The woman demanded. "I don't trust you, you always were a sneaky boy, and I know you lied to your mother!"

"All right," said Nicholas calmly. He took a small bottle from a pocket in his shirt. He had not mentioned it before, and I did not know he had it. He took out a small bowl from another pocket, and then poured some of the whiskey into it. He showed it to the woman, and then simply dumped it over the top of her skull on the edge of the circle. The woman smiled then and said "Ah, I feel it, I can taste it, that's good whiskey!" "Now the sigil or character," said Nicholas.

The woman looked at Nicholas from one eye, white hair hanging over the other eye. She looked drunk. All right, my character is the number 42," she said. Nicholas nodded, "good, you may go now" he said. The woman faded from view and the room was still and quiet. Nicholas turned to me. It is done, I have conjured the first ghost. We left the circle.

The work Begins

Now the work began in earnest. Nicholas and I spent many nights digging up skulls until there were 14 of them in the secret room. 7 ghosts for him, and 7 for me. With each ghost, we conjured it together and made a deal with it, gave it something in return for it giving us the sigils we needed. Some of the ghosts were friendly, some were sorrowful, and some were downright dark and evil, since three of the ghosts for Nicholas were those of hanged criminals.

Most of my ghosts were rather kind. They were departed family members, including my mother, father, grandmother, grandfather, and an aunt and uncle. Eventually all the ghosts were caught and bound to our service in some way.

Then it was time for the demons. I had been most interested in that part of the book and read it a hundred times. Since we had performed many conjurations of the dead, we were fully ready to summon demons when the time came. I will only recount one such experience here so that my readers may understand the scope and depth of such an experience. The spirit we had decided to summon was Asmodeus. Each of us had different demons. Asmodeus was the first one we called for me. Nicholas was in the circle with me but this time I was holding the wand. Nicholas lit the incense, and the smell of cherries filled the room.

I began the conjuration, but even as the words were barely in my mouth the demon appeared. He was standing upright on a fierce dragon. He held a spear in one hand and a flag or banner waved from the spear. He had three heads and looked like an ogre, with the other two heads being those of a man and a ram. The air grew hot around us, so much that I feared we had opened a doorway to hell. The voice of Asmodeus screamed at me.

"Fools, what gives you the power to summon me from my abode in the stars!" I shook. The ghosts had been nothing in comparison to this. I began to sweat. The force of his presence was so overwhelming I could not speak. "Speak!" He commanded me. I opened my mouth and tried to say that I wanted to become a magician, and I sought power. "I seek power" I said. "And why should I give it to you?" demanded the demon angrily. "Just because you want a thing, does not mean you can have it. What power or authority do you have to ask of me these things."

"Make a pact with me Asmodeus," I pleaded. "Show me what I must do in order to receive the gift of the demons, so that they must serve me, and I may succeed in my operation to become a werewolf." This was the first time I had spoken the words aloud. Suddenly the room was filled with many ghosts, there were many voices speaking at once. "How dare you?" said one male voice. "Flee this eternal damnation!" said another voice. "How could you?" another voice wailed. Nicholas and I swayed back and forth as the spirits surrounded us like a powerful wind, moving our bodies. It was all we could do to stand.

"Silence!" the demon screamed at the ghosts. All the ghosts in the room suddenly vanished and we were alone with the demon. Beams of red light shone around him then, and other demons like him flew erratically through the beams of light. I thought that the door to hell must be open, and I was looking directly into it. The demon looked at me fiercely. "To gain my power you must sell your soul to me, make a contract for all your life, that you will serve me in all your ways, giving no other demon your full allegiance. You must never enter a church or take communion with the Christians, always walking in the light of the Infernal regions. Swear now this oath."

"I swear it," I murmured, falling to my knees, and bowing my head. "So be it," the demon said, and then disappeared.

The oil of Transformation

At that point Nicholas and I worked together to create the oil. We purchased the herbs and ground them all into a powder slowly over the course of many days, all the while conjuring ghosts and demons. Once we had the powder, I mixed it with Alcohol to draw out the essence of the plants through my alchemy process. Once the pure essence of the plants was produced, I mixed the essence with olive oil rather than pig fat. I felt that this was much more modern, and less messy than slathering the body with the fat of a pig. My room truly became a wizards tower then, and the two of us became wizards. During this time, I spoke with no one other than Nicholas, and occasionally, the king, giving him updates on the books I had been reading in preparation to become an Alchemist.

And of course, sometimes Nicholas was there in the throne room telling the king about Astrology, which the old fool never seemed to grow bored with, and Nicholas was an expert at spinning yarns about this or that bit of astrological nonsense. All the while the two of us were working to prepare the oil of transformation. It took us three months to get it right. During this time, I only saw the queen once, in the throne room as I was speaking to the king about Alchemy, but she seemed not to notice me. This was for the better I supposed, and let the matter go.

Now I will tell you of the first transformation. It was Nicholas that decided we should go out into the woods. He said that if we transformed in the secret room, we might howl as wolves, and we would be discovered, but if we transformed in the woods, no one would notice. I agreed this was a good plan and let him lead the way. Nicholas knew the woods well and led us to a deserted spot. It was night, and the moon shone brightly above us. Nicholas took out the wand and used it to draw the magic circle in a clearing. Then he took out the skulls and placed them in their positions. He then drew the sigil of the demons in their places. We stripped off all our clothes and slathered the oil all over our bodies and tied on the wolfskins. By the time the wolf skins had been tied on the power of the oil began to take effect. Nicholas and I tried to say the words of invocation to the ghosts and demons, but we could barely speak.

Nicholas turned to me and gasped "do you see them?" I looked outside the circle and saw every sort of spiritual creature imaginable. Ghosts, demons, and even wolves, circling the place as if we were prey. "The wolves, they are going to eat us!" Nicholas grasped my shoulder with his hand in terror. "No, they won't, they are spirits," I replied. He took a deep breath and calmed down a little.

Suddenly before me I saw a point of red orange light, it seemed to hang in the air about 5 feet off the ground. "Look," I said to Nicholas and pointed at it. He looked. Then the point of light expanded, and it appeared like the magic circle we were standing in, except the symbols around the edges were different than any we had seen. This design hung in the air made of what looked like burning coals or red orange flame that shimmered and glowed softly. We stared at this shape, it was about 15 feet away from the magic circle, and perhaps 10 feet across.

As we looked at it, lights seem to come from within it, and rivers of fire swirled from it. This fire or light grew brighter and increased in its swirling motion until it seemed to blind us, and the whole area was lit up. Then from the center of it came a man, he stepped out of it as if coming through a doorway and it was as if he came out of another world and into ours.

He was dressed remarkably well, in the style of a king or great noble. He wore a green jacket with ornate orange flowers and unknown designs embroidered into it. Beneath this he had a white shirt with ruffles. He had a small thin bladed sword at his waist, and ornate rings on his fingers. His hair was white and tied back behind his head in a ponytail. As he stepped into our world and came towards us the door made of flame disappeared, fading into the darkness.

He walked towards us then, in the bright light of the moon. He came up to us calmly and said, "I am Marcus." I knew then that he was the one who had written the witch's book. I tried to look at his face. He had some quality about him that was terrifying. I could not determine if he was good or evil by my standards of judgment. I felt that he looked like no man I had ever seen, like someone from a painting or a storybook. There was something about him that told me he was from another time, another age, he was hundreds of years old, yet looked perhaps 65 or 70. Yet even old he had a power that shone through his look, his walk, his most subtle mannerisms, it was the power of a man who has no fear because he can crush all who oppose him.

He looked at us in a way that seemed like a king would look at his subjects. By some power unknown to us, Nicholas, and I both fell to the ground, howling like wolves, it was beyond our control to stop it. I saw hair growing all over me, at times I felt to be a man, and then I felt to be a wolf, and then I forgot I was a man, and then remembered I was a man. I can hardly describe these things here, for the power around us was so strong. We howled as wolves; I looked and saw Nicholas as a wolf. Then, there was a release like the thunder of a thousand orgasms. I heard a sound that sounded like a tree was splitting in half. It seemed as if the sound was inside me. It felt like I lost my form, and became small, and then I went through some sort of a long tunnel very fast, and then I was flying through the sky, and I saw darkness, and then stars being born in the sky, like balls of fire being ignited one by one. Then I was on my hands and knees again, in the magic circle and Marcus was standing over me and Nicholas.

He looked down at me and said, "you have done well, now run, and kill, and you will forever have the power, but first you must kiss the ring." He held out his hand as a king might and I saw a ring with a large purple stone on it, as I looked, it turned black, and then red like blood. As a wolf, I kissed the stone on his ring, and heard him say, "now go, what you seek is over there," he pointed out into the darkness to his right. An overwhelming power flowed through me, and I ran into the darkness of the forest, with no thought but to run, and to hunt, and to be alive under the stars.

After what seemed like an eternity of running, I came to a field. In the field were a herd of sheep. I ran into the herd at full speed and bit into the neck of one of the animals before any of them were awakened. At that moment, I tasted its blood, and an absolute fury came over me. It writhed in my grasp, still alive and kicking. The other sheep rose and scattered in all directions. I feasted on the sheep I had caught without any guilt, lost in the kill, like any wolf would be. The hot blood ran down my throat and was the most delicious thing ever.

Then I heard the screams of a human and shouting voices coming toward me. Somehow the owners of the sheep were awakened and were coming for me. I wanted to stay and finish my feast, but I knew that I must flee. It was then that I remembered I was a man. I looked down and realized that I was losing my wolf form. Instead of paws, I once again had hands, but they were covered in thick black hair. I was not yet a man, but not fully a wolf either, somewhere in between.

At that moment the farmer and his wife burst into the area with torches and pitchforks. The farmers wife looked and saw me then, in a human shape but covered in black hair blood running from my mouth, eyes like a demon. She screamed. The farmer ran towards me with his pitchfork, I stood up, but awkwardly fell backwards not being sure if I was a man or wolf. The farmer ran towards me and with a mighty yell stabbed at me with the pitchfork. I managed to crawl backwards a few feet as he was doing this, and instead of impaling my face or chest on the forks, one of them stabbed me in the foot. I screamed in pain and the sound came out in a way that was halfway between the sound of a man, and that of a wolf, it was an unnatural sound, not belonging to man or nature.

The farmer jumped back, holding on to the pitchfork tightly and raising it up in defense. I turned over in one swift movement, and began to run on all fours, like a wolf, yet in the shape of a hairy man. I ran into the darkness and quickly left the farmer and his wife behind. As I ran, I found that I fully became a wolf again. I knew I needed to return to the magic circle because that was where my clothes were. Finally, I found it. When I passed into the magic circle, the wolf form fell away and I was once again a man. I looked down and found that the wound on my foot had disappeared. Nicholas was nowhere in sight, nor was Marcus. I wondered if he had returned to the other world.

I gathered up the skulls and put them in a bag. I also collected the cherry wood wand, and with my foot, I blurred the lines drawn in the dirt for the magic circle. I left the clothes of Nicholas behind hoping he would find them. I knew that soon it would be sunrise and I must get back into my room. As quickly as I could, I returned to my wizard's tower. Once I had safely returned home and placed the magical tools in the secret room, I fell fast into a deep sleep.

The wolf is on the loose

The next day, I received word that the king wished to see me. I went to the throne room and found it in an uproar. The king was in one corner of the room talking to Nicholas and two other men I did not know the names of. As I approached, I heard parts of their conversation. "And you say the woman was torn apart?" The king asked one of the men. Nicholas was crying. I could not believe my eyes. What could he possibly be so upset about?

I approached the throne cautiously where the king and queen sat. The queen was quiet but listening intensely to the conversation. I joined the group silently. "My own mother!" Nicholas sobbed. "What is going on?" I asked. All around the room people spoke in hushed whispers.

The king rolled his eyes at my question. "The people say that there has been a werewolf attack, but I do not believe in such superstitious nonsense." "What happened?" I asked. "They say that a farmer and his wife have stated that last night a werewolf killed one of their sheep, they came upon the werewolf in the process of this happening, and the farmer still has blood on his pitchfork, which he is showing to the others in his village. His wife claims to have seen the beast as well. It is said to have escaped into the forest."

Nicholas sobbed pitifully. I felt sorry for him. "Also," said a man near the king, a woman was killed in the forest, and torn apart as if by a wolf. It hit me then, the woman killed was the mother of Nicholas. This was shocking. My mind tried to process these developments. I knew that the monster the farmer had stabbed with his pitchfork had been me. Thankfully my wound had miraculously healed. Had a werewolf really killed that woman? If so, who could it be? Had Marcus done it while he was in our world. Or were there other werewolves out there? Then it hit me... Nicholas! No, it could not be, I did not want to believe it, surely, he would not do such a thing. Or would he?

I looked over at Nicholas, he looked like a man in deep sorrow, his eyes were bloodshot, and he was wiping tears from his eyes.

The king looked at me. "Valentius," he said, "do you believe in werewolves?" "I... I don't know sir, I have never given it any thought, it is not within the realm of my study." The king frowned "But surely you have read the book, the one from the trial of those witches many months ago, does it say anything which might give us a way to know if there might be werewolves, and if so, how to identify them and find them?"

He seemed genuinely concerned, although he had stated previously that he did not believe in the existence of werewolves. At that moment I caught the queen looking at me. She turned away quickly, but I had the feeling that she was remembering when I had read the book to her. I guessed that the king was not aware of her visits to my room, or that she knew the contents of the witch's book. I felt important then because I was being considered as someone who might know things about magic, and werewolves. The king and the queen waited for me to reply.

"Well, it says in the book that those who wish to be werewolves must conjure the spirits of 7 ghosts, so if there really is a werewolf in these parts, and they have carried out the spell in the book, they will have probably done some digging in the graveyard, to uncover the skulls of the souls they wish to conjure." I said this with great seriousness and self-importance, as one who knows. I could tell the king was impressed. He turned to one of the men standing nearby and told them to search all the graveyards in the area looking for signs that they had been disturbed.

"What else," the king asked. "Well, the book demands that the witch who uses it make a wand from a cherry tree. It might be hard to find, but if there was seen a branch of a cherry tree that had been recently cut, it might point to someone carrying out the work of the book." "Have there ever been other books of this nature found?" I asked. "Oh yes, many," the king said absentmindedly, they are held in the house of the inquisitor, in a library of banned books. "Might I look at these books?" I asked. If I could see other spell books written by witches and werewolves, I might be able to learn more about if these creatures do exist, so that we may catch them."

"I can see how this might be helpful to your study." The king stated. "I command you now to gather all the books taken from witches by the inquisition and take them to your library. You will learn all you can on this subject and report to me of what you find in the hopes that if there really is a werewolf out there, we may identify it and catch it before it kills again."

The king turned to Nicholas and said "Nicholas, go with Valentius to the house of the inquisitor and tell him that the king has stated that all the spell books taken from witches are to be given to Valentius. He turned to another man and directed him to go with us as well and carry the authority of the king and his words to the Inquisitor.

The three of us went to the house of the inquisitor. He was an evil looking man who I guessed had tortured many witches to get them to confess crimes which would in the end lead to their execution. His house was large and wealthy. It was filled with crosses and paintings of Christ dying on the cross, and demons dragging unfortunate sinners to hell. We walked past torture devises such as the Iron Maiden, to a wall filled with the most demonic books you could imagine. Some of them were bound in the skins of animals such as snakes and wolves, or even possibly men who had been hanged.

The kings man stated to the Inquisitor that we were to take all these books. He gave us a foul look but did not deny us. It took the three of us several trips to gather the 153 books of magic. They were taken to my room and over the course of the next day I catalogued them and began to try and understand them.

After the king's man had left me and Nicholas alone, Nicholas changed into a happy person and cheerfully asked me what had happened when I ran into the woods. I told him the story of how I had been stabbed by the farmer and healed in a miraculous manner. "So that was you!" Nicholas laughed. I asked him what happened to him. He explained that Marcus had told him to run in the opposite direction as me. He had run for what seemed like an eternity and then he came to a cabin in the woods. He recognized it as the home that he grew up in and wanted to explore it. When he had opened the door to the place, he saw that it was not deserted, but a low fire burned in the hearth and a woman was sleeping in a rocking chair in one corner. The woman woke up and to his surprise, it was his mother. She had fallen asleep drunk in the chair. Nicholas said that he knew immediately that he wanted to kill her. He said that he went over to her and shook her awake. It was very hard to do because she was still drunk, but finally she woke up. He told me that when she woke up, he was in his form of half human half wolf, and somehow, she recognized him despite his ferocious appearance. "And then I ate her!" Nicholas said happily.

I stared at him in horror, "So it was you…" "Yes," said Nicholas, he didn't seem in the least bit disturbed by this and was in fact happy. He saw my look and said "oh come on, she deserved it, she was awful to me as a child. Once she kneeled on my chest and beat me while screaming bible verses at me. If I had a gold piece for every time that woman told me I was a horrible child and going to hell, I would be richer than the king."

I did not know what to say. I did not know what his childhood had been like, perhaps his mother did beat him every day, perhaps she did deserve to die, how could I know? "Ok," I said, "but you're not going to kill anyone else, right?" "I don't know, maybe I will," said Nicholas

with a smile, "If I want to I will, after all, I am a werewolf."
But Nicholas, we can't go around doing what we did last
night, we will get found out, get caught, and hanged or
burned at the stake," I pleaded with him. "That's true,"
said Nicholas, we have to be careful now, most people
won't believe in werewolves, but there will be some who
do." "Isn't it funny that we are the ones who are
supposed to be looking for the werewolves? And we are
the werewolves!" He laughed and laughed. Eventually I
had to smile a little, the situation was strange.

Return of the Queen

The next day the Queen returned to my room. She
wanted to know what I had found out about werewolves
from the books I had taken from the Inquisitor. I said that
I had not yet studied them as I had only received them the
day before. The Queen began to press me for more
information on Werewolves, she asked me to read the
witches book to her again and I did so. When I was done
there was silence, and then she plainly asked me if I
would like to become a werewolf. I pretended that such a
thing would be unthinkable, but then I realized that she
herself was entertaining the idea. I wanted to continue
the conversation and I boldly asked her if she would
consider such a thing. "No...Yes" she said. She looked at
me then and smiled so sweetly that I lost my reserve and
began to trust her a little. "And what would you do as a
werewolf?" I asked.

"I suppose I would be free, to go wherever I wished, and do whatever I wished, and eat whoever I wished." She laughed then and I laughed with her.

"What would you do as a werewolf?" She asked me. I paused and thought about it. "Well, I suppose I would be a good werewolf," I answered. She laughed at me, and I continued. "The book says that werewolves live an unnaturally long time, and I would use my long life to become a master of Alchemy, and magic, and perhaps even learn to play musical instruments. Maybe I would build a castle, and gather all the best books there, and make hundreds of experiments of magic. That's what I would do."

"That sounds wonderful," she said and reached out to me and touched my hand gently. It was a small gesture, and appropriate for the moment, our eyes met, and we both looked away and smiled. Somewhere deep down I knew that it was inappropriate for her to be here and to have been talking with me so much. What would the king think if he knew? That caused me some apprehension and I straightened in my chair and drew back from her a little.

She seemed to notice this and said, "He doesn't have to know… about us." My emotions went through all sorts of ups and downs then, I felt guilt and desire mixed, and pride that she was admitting feelings for me. "Valentius, the king does not fulfill…my desires." She said quietly, "and you do." "My Queen," I said in a heavy voice, almost gasping for air. It was useless, I wanted her, and I could not stop myself. In that moment I knew that I would take the risk of taking her.

"Valentius, show me the way you did it," she said. I jolted and looked at her "did what?" I asked, even though I knew what she was asking. "I know its you," she said, you are the werewolf, and so is Nicholas probably, but I don't want him." "My Queen…." I stammered, surely you don't think I…" "I do think…she said quietly, I think it must be you, you have the witch's book, you know it better than anyone else, and you told me that Nicholas had it for a while too, it must be one of you, or both of you. Give me the secret." She got out of her chair and came toward me. I was sitting in a chair, and she climbed on top of me. She leaned forward and her breasts were in my face. She smelled like roses; she caressed the side of my face. "Valentius…" she murmured. She kissed me on the lips and rubbed her hand gently across my chest as she straddled me. "Valentius…" she moaned, my darling, my lover… tell me the secret. How did you do it?" My desire for her felt like thunder pounding in my veins.

At that moment the door opened, and the Queens attendant stood in the doorway looking nervous. "My Queen," she said hastily, someone comes!" The Queen jumped off me in a flash, and at that moment Nicholas came into the room through the open door. He stood beside the queens' attendant, looking at me, and then the queen, and then at her attendant as if trying to understand what was happening. The queen looked at me, then at Nicholas, and then without a word grabbed the hand of her attendant and swept from the room quickly.

When they were gone, Nicholas quietly shut the door and faced me. "What the hell was that?" He asked me suspiciously. I sighed, "The Queen is on to us, apparently, she is not as stupid as her husband and has guessed that we are the werewolves. She tried to seduce me to get the secret out of me, she just kissed me." I said it with a mix of pride and confusion, the whole thing had happened so fast. The feeling of desire was still warm on my skin and so was the smell of roses. "You are going to get us both killed!" Nicholas said angrily. "I warned you about all of this, I told you not to trust a woman, all they ever do is lie, and nothing they ever say can be trusted in any way. You think the Queen wants you? Who the hell are you? She is the Queen, she is rich, and beautiful, and she could make any man want her if that's what game she is going to play. How the hell do you think she got to be Queen? She seduced that old fool king just the way she did you, you can't stand up against her powers, she has played with you since the very start!"

I did not know what to say, I could find no way to argue with him, and believed he was probably right, but at the same time, I was spellbound by the Queens affections, and I did not know how to stop myself from feeling the desire I had for her, as well as the way it was flattering to think that she might find me attractive. I thought of our conversations about the books of Alchemy. I remembered us laughing together, and I wanted to believe she loved me.

Adding to my feelings of confusion were that Nicholas was my friend, and that I was bound to keep his secrets and he mine. "We must keep each other's secrets, Nicholas had said when this all began, and I had agreed. I wanted to be a man of honor. I wanted to be a good friend even, but I was torn. "I didn't tell her anything Nicholas," I stated truthfully. "Oh, but you will," he said scornfully. "She will be back, and she will work it out of you one way or the other." I knew this was true. And the fact that I did not deny it caused Nicholas to accuse me of it again. I was silent for a moment.

"Let's bring her in," I said. If she becomes a werewolf, she will have to keep the secret. Nicholas looked away. I could tell he did not like the idea, but he did not immediately dismiss it either because I think he could see that, yes, she would know our secret, but also, we would know hers. He paced around the room as I sat calmly in the chair. I liked this idea, and it seemed the solution to our dilemma. "Well, that's your business, you teach her then," said Nicholas, I want no part of it." I took a deep breath. "I will show her, I will teach her the way.

You better get something out of it too!" Nicholas said angrily, "Make her fuck you for it." "Take her out in the woods and rub the oil all over her and give it to her good. That will make her a werewolf!" I had to admit his idea was appealing to me and laughed. I thought about making love to the Queen with a wolfskin tied to her body. "But what about the ghosts? The demons, the whole process?" "The Queen is not going to go about doing all that stuff we did," said Nicholas, "There is no way she is going to dig up the skulls of 7 ghosts and learn how to conjure demons. But that doesn't matter, because you already did all that, you can draw the circle, and conjure your ghosts and demons, and they will come and bring the power." "And Marcus?" I asked. "He will come from the other world and make her kiss the ring if she changes, of that, I am sure," said Nicholas.

"Why did he do that?" I wondered aloud. "I don't know," said Nicholas, "but I think its his way of showing us he is the king of werewolves, or the current ruler, the book says there was a woman before him, but it does not say her name." "That's true," I nodded.

Nicholas then turned to me and said that it was up to me to handle the Queen. "You take care of it; I have other things to care about. I want to test my powers tonight. Tonight, I hunt. Then he left the room without saying another word. I wondered if he was going to hunt an animal, or a human. "What have I done?" I thought. Nicholas is a monster. And what of the Queen? What sort of werewolf would she be? But I couldn't turn back then, I was in too deep.

The Queens Garden

The Queen's Gardens was a magnificent place. I tell you that the king of France in that day had great wealth, but there is no way to fully describe it. On one side of the Palace was a vast garden, built for the Queen, perhaps 100 acres of land that had been meticulously cleaned and transformed into a world of its own. I can hardly describe its beauty on a summer day. All through the garden were placed benches for sitting and conversation, and these gardens were only for Royals. The entire area was surrounded by fencing which was filled with vines and ivy. Walking paths led under great oak trees. Streams meandered through some areas. Thousands of flowers of all colors were planted within the garden. In many places the shrubs had been pruned to make hedges and might surround a bench or path so that there was almost a maze of walking paths.

Yet also, there was a lot of sunshine. I remember the way the sun shined into the garden was almost like heaven on earth. It was to this garden that I was called by the Queen. I heard her calling my name. "Valentius…" She must be somewhere ahead of me. I walked along the paths. "Valentius, come to me, my lover…" Her voice was soft and pleading. I felt desire rise in me for her, I wanted to take her. Then I rounded a corner and saw her sitting on a bench alone. The Queen!

I walked up to her. The sun shone through the trees in such a beautiful way, and the birds sang. As I got close to her, she turned towards me. I stopped, there was a different look in her eye, something had changed about her. Her black hair was piled high upon her head, and she wore a black dress with purple flowers embroidered all over it. She looked so beautiful. The birds stopped singing. Her eyes, they looked different, like that of a dog, all black. I looked down and saw the pale white skin of her neck and then suddenly black hair grew on it, her face began to transform into that of a wolf, just enough that I knew that she was a werewolf, and then she was once again only a woman, but I knew, I knew she had changed, she was a werewolf now.

I heard the shouts of children playing in the distance. Perhaps someone in the royal family was having a picnic. Suddenly I thought to myself how here in this beautiful garden was this monstrous evil, this werewolf before me. I feared for the children. She looked at me as if she somehow knew what I was thinking. "But why shouldn't we eat the little ones?" she asked. "No..." I gasped, "no, leave them be." She smiled and as she did so her faced changed from woman to wolf. My horror was beyond words. "I made you this way!" I cried in agony. "What have I done?"

In that moment I woke in my bed. The sun shined through the window and a few birds chirped in the distance. I realized my visions of seeing the Queen in the Garden was only a dream. It had felt so real. I lay there thinking about what was before me. I had to make the Queen a werewolf, so that she would keep my secret, but what then? She would have the power, what would she do with it? What did Nicholas do last night? Did he hunt, did he kill again? I had the feeling he did, and this would only increase the fears of the people and their belief in a werewolf.

I jumped up from my bed, I had better get to studying the books I had taken from the Inquisitor and learn something to tell the king, give him some bit of interesting information so that he would find me useful. Suddenly I realized that I did not want to be in the palace any longer, I did not want to spend the rest of my life serving some petty king and making Alchemical experiments to amuse him as Nicholas filled him with astrological foolishness about his supposed place in the grand scheme of things. I wanted a way out of all of this.

I sat at my table and began to furiously read the books I had taken from the inquisitor. Most of them were designed to conjure the four sorts of spirits known in that day which were angels, demons, fairies, and ghosts. Some of the books also had spells for doing such things as causing love, healing sick farm animals, driving away a pesky neighbor, finding treasure and the like. I read book after book looking for information on werewolves.

Finally, I came across another book which was designed to make a man or woman into a werewolf, it was called the grimoire of Moyset. The basic principles were the same, there was an oil to be made from plants, the wearing of the skin of a wolf, but this time, instead of a long process of conjuring demons and ghosts, there was an invocation to the dark lord of the Forest, a man or devil called Moyset. This was called "the Grand Operation."

There were also several other smaller spells for becoming a wolf. Some seemed to be only bits of folklore, such as "If you drink rainwater from the paw print of a wolf, you will become a wolf on the next full moon, and every full moon thereafter."

Three books later I came across a strange bit of folklore. The writer of the book claimed to be the son of the legendary magician Faust, something I doubted as the book was written in French rather than German. At the end of the book, there was a short section on magical beasts such as the unicorn and the Chimera. After this the author wrote...

"It is said by some that there is a dark and evil method of becoming a werewolf by the magical art, or rather by a trick of sorts. He or she who would become a werewolf must know the habits of wolves very well and leave them a gift of a sheep tied to a pole or left in a place where they will find it and kill it. Then that person must go and drive away the wolves from the body by whatever means they can, and then take the dead sheep home and clean it and cook it and eat it. It is believed that they will be possessed by the spirit of the wolf, and at various times they will change, though it can never be determined when."

The writer of the book then went on to say that "there are some witches who have sought this power by the means of potions made from plants or mushrooms, or certain flowers, roots, or barks. Other witches say the gift can only come from the devil, and that he gives the form of wolves to his witches at the Sabbath, and from there they go out to hunt and kill among the sheep. And it is said that there are also certain magical pools and streams where when one swims, they may become wolves."

I wondered about these things if they had any truth to them. I wondered if there were any other werewolves out there in the world besides me and Nicholas, for Marcus could hardly be said to exist in this world, though he could enter it. At least these bits of information would sound important if I was called before the king to tell him what I had learned about werewolves. I was weary of this game already. Here I knew exactly who the werewolves were that the king and his men were looking for, and I was pretending to give him information from my research to help fix the problem.

Then there was a knock on the door, it was an attendant of the king calling for me. I grabbed the book I had just been reading and put it in my pocket and went quickly to the throne room. There I found a distressing scene. Once again Nicholas stood by the king in an apparent state of shock, weeping. As I approached the king, I saw the Queen sitting beside him. She did not look at me. "There has been another attack," the king stated quickly, this time, the victim was a young boy in a stable grooming a horse. His mother heard him screaming and came to the scene in time to see the werewolf rip out the poor boy's heart. She fainted, and perhaps the werewolf would have killed her too, but at that time the boy's uncle and father came upon the scene and with swords drove the werewolf away."

"The boy was my young cousin!" Sobbed Nicholas. I knew that the werewolf had to be Nicholas again, yet he was playing the part of a broken-hearted family member once again to perfection. I started to feel sorry for him, and then realized what utter foolishness this was. What sort of grudge did he have toward the boy? Was it revenge, or just the sheer hunger of the beast that drove him to do it? I remembered hunting the lamb I had killed, and I wanted to hunt again, but I had no desire to kill any one from my earlier life, I had no thoughts of revenge in me, no bitterness. For a split second, the Queen caught my eye, and I knew that she knew. She had to guess the one who was doing the killings was Nicholas.

"Have you learned anything more from the books taken from those who practice this evil art?" The king asked me. "Yes, there are some small things, it takes time to read through so many books, but I can tell you that there are various ways I have discovered that one might become a werewolf," I told this to the king in a quiet voice. "For instance, it is believed that one may become a werewolf by drinking rainwater from the pawprint of a wolf," I said. "It is also believed that there are certain streams and rivers which, when bathed in, one might transform. And there are types of roots, flowers, herbs, and mushrooms which are prepared into pastes and then rubbed on the skin. Sometimes the witch might combine several of these methods or spells until they have success." The king listened attentively, and I continued. "It is also believed that the devil gives the wolfskin to some witches at the Sabbath."

The king seemed shocked by this. "How many witches of this sort do you think could be within my kingdom?" He asked me gravely. I didn't know. I told the king that I needed more time to study the books and he seemed satisfied with this answer and dismissed me.

The Queen transforms

The next day the Queen came to my room again. She demanded that I tell her if I was the werewolf or if Nicholas was. She said that she would give me anything for the secret, even her body. She kissed me again and I wanted her badly. Finally, I confessed that Nicholas and I had accomplished it, and that Nicholas had done the killings out of revenge. "He has become a monster," I told her, and then asked her "What will you become? Why do you want this?" "I just want to be free," she said, "to wander in the woods, and to fear nothing, and to not have to answer to the whims of that feeble old king." I looked at her and tried to judge what sort of werewolf she would be, but I could not read her, she was too fast for me, always changing the expression on her face, always playing with me.

"I will give you the power," I said, but you must give me a treasure." "And how can I do that?" She asked. "I don't know, perhaps you will have to steal it," I responded. "But I know that you can, I want to leave this place someday, and build that castle I told you about, a place where I too can be free." "Oh, that sounds wonderful," she said. "Can I come live with you there?" I laughed. "How will you do that if you are the Queen?" I felt she was only playing with me. "Well, perhaps I can come visit you in your castle someday" she told me.

"And what about my body? Don't you want me?" She leaned towards me then and caressed my face and kissed me. I remembered what Nicholas had said about how I should demand to fuck her in exchange for the knowledge of how to become a werewolf. I wanted to take her then and there, and my blood pounded in my ears. "I want you," I said, "but not that way, you must give yourself to me willingly. For the power of the wolf, you will give me gold, and diamonds, a true treasure." "Oh, I will," she said to me, "I will, I can command my servant to take gold from the treasury and I can give you my very crown. I will say it was stolen, and no one will be able to say otherwise."

I thought of the Queens Garden and my dream from the night before. "You will give me the treasure, and then the next night you must sneak away and come with me into the woods, and there I will show you the way to become a werewolf," I told her. "It will be done," she said. "I will send my attendant with the crown and the gold late tonight, and then tomorrow night I will say that I cannot sleep and wish to walk in the garden, then we will go to the forest so that you can give me the power." With these plans made, she left me.

That evening Nicholas came to my room, and I told him of my plans and what we had agreed. He only nodded and shrugged his shoulders. I asked him about the boy he had killed, and he confessed to me. He had no guilt for his awful deed and said that the boy had been mean to him and so he deserved what he got, and that his heart had been delicious. We talked for some time and then he left to go to his room. Late that night the attendant of the Queen arrived with a bag of gold and the queen's crown. It was made of gold and covered in precious stones. It was worth a fortune, a treasure indeed. After she was gone, I took it out into the woods and buried it. Thus, even Nicholas did not know where it was.

The next night the time had come for the Queen to transform. She came to my room alone this time and we hurried out into the darkness of the forest. I took her to the same place Nicholas, and I had become werewolves. I drew the magic circle and conjured the spirits. She was in awe when the spirits came, flying around the circle like so many bats. "Oh Valentius, its real, at last I see!" "Take off all your clothes," I ordered. "Are we going to make love?" she asked. "No, you must get the oil on your skin." She took all her clothes off and I helped her rub the oil all over her body and tie on the wolf skin. It was the first time I had seen her naked, and it greatly pleased me. She was beautiful like I had never imagined.

"The Lord of the forest will come when it is time." I told her. "I feel so strange" she said, "and the colors, they are like a rainbow of snowflakes." "What do you see?" I asked her then. "I see wolves, they are all around the circle, one of them has jumped inside me, its inside me now, I feel my body changing." I looked at her, she was growing hair all over her at an astonishing speed. "The Lord of the Forest, the Master will come, and you must swear obedience to him, and kiss his ring," I told her. "Look for a point of light."

It was then that the doorway appeared, it looked like the magic circle, with a star inside, two points upward. Around the edges were the sigils of demons and ghosts. Once again, I saw Marcus come through the door. He was dressed as before with a green jacket and red pants, his long white hair pulled back. He approached us again as before looking at me and looking at her. I was once again afraid of him, I could not tell if he was good or evil, he just seemed cold, merciless. He walked up to the Queen, and he held out his hand, the stone upon his ring reflected the moonlight. "Kiss the ring," he told the Queen. Without a word she did so. He stretched out his hand and pointed into the darkness. He looked down at the Queen and spoke to her, "go, and kill, and you will have the power forever." She howled an inhuman howl and then ran into the darkness.

Marcus turned and walked toward the doorway. "Wait" I shouted at him. I wanted to talk to him, know something of who or what he was. "I go where you cannot, my son," he said in a calm voice. "Where do you go?" I asked him. "Into the world of spirits, the other side," he said simply. "Why can't I go there?" I asked him. "Because you have not yet saved enough power." "Can you teach me the way to do this?" I asked him. "No, he replied, it is something that will come to you over the years, it is similar to having wisdom, no man can give that to another man, it can only be learned alone." "When were you born?" I asked him. "In the year 952, as you count years," he told me. I was shocked. He turned to go.

"Will I ever see you again?" I asked him. "Yes, someday you will become like me, you are my heir to this knowledge, and someday you will become the Master as I now am. But don't worry about that now." He looked at me and then said "you think you wanted to become a werewolf; you think you found my book, but that is not so. It was I who found you, it is I who brought the book to you, and it is I who directs your steps, from the other world where I can travel at the speed of thought." I was overwhelmed by this knowledge. "Master..." I reached out my hand towards him as he entered the door and disappeared. Then I found myself alone in the forest.

I quickly gathered the magic wand and the skulls and my jar of werewolf oil and went to the castle. Whatever happened now, I was free. I realized I didn't need the skulls anymore; I was not going to make any more werewolves. Whatever happened with the queen, I was free of the castle. I used my werewolf skills to sneak into a barn and steal a shovel. I found an abandoned cemetery and buried the skulls and the magic wand and the bottle of oil. I wanted to go back to my tower then and make plans to leave, take the treasure I had received from the Queen and buy a house in the country somewhere, to get away from the pressures of the court. I did not want to work for the king anymore, and I had found a way to be free.

Death of the King

When I returned to the palace, it was in an uproar. People ran to and fro in all directions. I stopped someone and asked, "What is the meaning of this?" "The werewolf has killed again, this time it was the queen's attendant!" My God, I thought, it must have been the Queen herself, that was her first kill. The person I had stopped ran in the other direction, and I headed for the throne room. Torches and lamps had been lit and men stood around in armor holding spears and swords.

I wandered toward the throne room, hearing bits of conversation from people who passed me. "The woman's body was found in the Queens Garden just after midnight, she was torn apart!" Another voice said, "The Queen herself is missing." I wandered numbly through the corridors towards the throne room. "What have I done?" I thought. "This is all because of me, I asked for the book, I led Nicholas into it, he would never have tried it on his own, and now his mother and cousin are dead, and the queen's attendant is dead, and I am sure there will be many more deaths to come."

The words of Marcus rang in my ears "You think you wanted to be a werewolf, but I chose you." How could that be so? Was Marcus some sort of god or devil now? Or something different, all in its own category. I came into the throne room; the king noticed me coming and waved me over towards him. Nicholas stood to his right, looking wild eyed, and there were also many soldiers and important looking men in the group. They were gathered around a table which had been brought into the room and upon which was placed a map of the palace grounds.

"Our first priority is to find the queen," the king said. He gestured to the map and commanded the soldiers to search each part of the palace systematically. "The body was found here," he pointed to a place on the map, "in the Queens gardens." Men left to look for the Queen. "The king turned to me and said "Valentius, it appears that the werewolf is real. My men tell me that the poor girls head was almost bitten off and her heart was ripped out. No man could do that, we must face the truth that we are dealing with a werewolf. I fear that the werewolf may have taken my Queen and is now feasting on her entrails somewhere deep in the forest."

At that moment the two doors leading to the throne room were thrown open and the Queen walked in. There was a gasp all around the room as she walked boldly up to where we were standing. She was barefoot, wearing a red dress which was torn, and one of the straps over her shoulder was missing. Her hair hung wildly from her head and bits of bark and dirt was in her hair and fell from her dress. "My king..." she said sweetly as she approached. There was a wild look in her eyes. Everyone standing around the king took a step back. For her to look and act in this way was unthinkable. "I have found the werewolf!" she stated triumphantly. "What?" startled murmurs around the room could be heard. "Is that so?" The king asked slowly. "Yes, yes," the queen assured him boldly. "The werewolf is right here in this room..." She looked around the throne room at the two dozen or so people who stood there taking time to look at me and Nicholas. "Yes..., go on," the king said.

The Queen looked slowly around the room, the court seemed to shrink back from her gaze, afraid of being accused of such an awful crime. The Queen walked up to the king and reached out her hand and caressed the side of his head. "Yes, my king, I have found the werewolf and it is me." She changed then, her face becoming that of a wolf, her hands with terrible claws. The king had no chance, he was drawn towards her by the strength of her arms, and she bit into his throat and tore it out before anyone in the room could do anything.

Screams erupted around the room and there was total chaos and panic as people ran for the doors. The kings guard jumped back and drew their weapons. They dared not attack her. She dragged the king's body toward the throne, and at the steps leading up to the throne ripped out his heart and ate it. She then ripped off her dress and sat in her throne naked in her human form, with blood still dripping from her mouth. It was the most awful spectacle I have ever seen. Even the guards of the king were so terrified they ran from the room and barred the doors leaving the queen, me, and Nicholas, alone in the room.

"Oh, its lovely Valentius!" She said to me. "I love it, I love the tase of his blood, I just took him like he took me so many times, like a beast." She kicked the lifeless body of the king with one naked foot. "How does it feel?" She yelled at him. "Is this what you wanted?" I said to her, "Well you got it." I heard voices outside the door, I knew that soon there would be dozens of armed men to come in and then what? "You can't fight them all!" I told her. "Oh really? I bet I could." She stated calmly and smiled.

I knew there was only one way out of this room, and that was through a nearby stained-glass window. I threw a chair through it and turned to Nicholas, "come on, let's go." I looked at the Queen. "You can't fight them all." Then I jumped through the window with Nicholas not far behind. We landed in a moat and began to swim. It was dark, I turned around while swimming and looked over my shoulder, I did not see the Queen, but it looked like the palace was on fire now, with flames coming from the windows. I wondered if she had escaped, or if she had died fighting. Why? Why would she do all this? Perhaps to her that was the ultimate freedom. Where would she go now?

Nicholas and I reached the bank. "Nicholas," I gasped, I am leaving this place. The king is dead, and I don't want to be here any longer." "Where will you go?" Nicholas asked me. I don't know, perhaps I will live like a bear in a cave for a while, but I must find some place to hide my books." "Do you even need them now?" He asked me, we have this power for life." "Yes, I know, but there are still things I would like to try from them, and I just love them, I will save them." "What about you?" I will go to the house of my dead mother and live there for a while, and then work towards a new plan I have been thinking of." "Perhaps come and visit me someday?" It was a question. "Ok Nicholas, I will, someday, goodbye for now."

We parted then and I made my way to my tower. I put all my books into boxes and lowered them down to the ground with a rope. Then I set my wizards tower on fire as well, so that no one would know what had happened to the books or me. The king was dead, and anyone else who had known me would probably think I had died in the fire. By this time the whole palace was on fire. I dragged my chest full of books into the woods. I stole two horses from a nearby farm and loaded them down with the books and my treasure. Then I made my way deep into the country, looking back to see the palace burning behind me.

After I had traveled at least 50 miles from the palace I had once called home, I found and bought a small house and set up my library there, it was not much, just a simple house in the woods, but I could build my castle there over time.

Then one day I received a visit from the Queen…

The Story of Peter Stubbe, Last Word, and Testament

THE FIGHT AND THE FISHING TRIP

I Peter Stubbe write this story as my last will and testament, for I am sure that I am soon to be tortured and cruelly put to death. My only hope is that my son has found the wolfskin belt, and that he will reach the Hertzberg mountains, and someday, Valhalla. It also my wish that the traitor of our kind, Magistrate Remy, be exposed for his treachery, and that his name be remembered in shame, for all his days. May he be hunted by the Inquisition, and the fate that he has planned for me come upon him.

Where shall I begin? I have only three days to tell my tale, as at the end of that time, I am sure to be executed for the crime of Werewolfery. Let me start at the beginning. When I became a Werewolf, I was only a boy of 12 years old. My uncle was of the society of wolves and led me to the dark Lord. I remember he used to make certain comments from time to time about how some people did not believe that a man could become a wolf, but that it was so, and then he would look at me with a certain kind of look, as if sizing up my character. I knew that my uncle ran with a crowd of people who might be considered criminals, and that sometimes they acted nearly in the manner of savage wolves, fighting and yelling. Sometimes they were covered in dirt and scratches as if they had been running through the forest as wolves. But I never believed any of it meant that they could really become wolves.

At the age of 11, I got into a fight with some boys who were bigger than me. Even though they beat me severely and bloodied my lip, my uncle did nothing to help me. He just stood nearby watching. The boys knocked me down, but I did not want them to make me cry, I wanted to be a man. So, I kept getting back up to fight, and kept getting knocked down. Finally, I could not get up to fight anymore. The boys grew bored and went away. My uncle picked me up by the neck and said that we should go fishing, and that he wanted me to meet a friend of his. He gathered a few supplies and we set out, me mostly limping along. As we passed the trail that led to the place where we normally fished, my uncle said he knew of another place, further along, that might have bigger fish. I was in no condition to argue, so on we went.

We walked for a long time and further than I had ever been from the village. Eventually, the sun began to go down, and we had not reached the place to fish. My uncle said not to worry, it would be just ahead. Finally, as the sun was setting, we came to an opening in the path where before us was a portion of the river, I do not remember which one, I was only 11, or perhaps 12. The sun seemed to be going down quickly now, and my uncle suggested that we make camp and do some fishing in the morning. So, we did, we made camp, and ate some dried fruits and meat, and drank a tea that he made. It had a somewhat bitter taste, and I did not like it very much, but my uncle said that was good for my health and would give me strength for the long walk home, and fishing the next day, so I drank it. After a while I fell asleep.

Sometime during the night, it seemed that I woke up, or was dreaming, I had the curious sensation that I could not tell which. The fire had died down, and the full moon hung over the water casting a soft glow. I was suddenly shocked to see that my body seemed to still be lying on the ground, asleep. I held up my hands and looked at them, they seemed to look the same, but had a slight sparkle to them. I then noticed that my uncle had risen and put a few logs on the fire. He then sat quietly by the fire for some time. I watched this scene until it seemed that I wanted to look at the moon. It was large, and beautiful. As I looked at it, it seemed to grow even larger. Suddenly I heard the howl of a wolf from a long distance away. "I must wake up!" I thought to myself frantically. I looked to my uncle to see if he had heard the sound. He had. He stared into the distance and seemed to be waiting for something. The howl sounded again, closer. I grew frantic. "Why did I not wake up?" My uncle stood and yelled into the night "Valentius!"

A few moments later I was terrified to see the form of a large gray wolf step into the glow of the firelight. I then experienced complete and total terror such as I had never known. I looked over at my body in one last feeble attempt to wake up, but there seemed to be no connection between my body and my soul. As I stared at the wolf, it seemed that there was an opening in its chest, and the hair of it was suddenly drawn back as if by some force and split apart, as if one were opening curtains made of hair, and the wolf skin fell away, and there was suddenly a man standing there. I knew then that I must be dreaming, and some of my fright left me. The man was old, perhaps twice as old as my uncle or more. He was standing completely naked and unashamed, with long gray hair hanging about his shoulders, and scattered around his chest.

His eyes looked black or perhaps a dark blue, and they shone brightly in the firelight. He regarded my uncle with an air of superiority and power, as if my uncle were nothing to him. He spoke, "I take it this is the boy you brought me?" "Why is he sleeping?" "One would think he would have woken up with all your yelling. You could have summoned me with a whisper, you fool." His tone was cutting. "I...I... yes." My uncle stammered. "Who is he to you?" The man asked. "He is my nephew" my uncle said plainly. "And yet you would sacrifice him to me?" The man said, with a touch of bite in his voice. My uncle hesitated, as if he did not know the right answer. "Yes, my Lord." He said slowly a note of fear creeping into his voice. "Why is he sleeping?" The man asked again. "I gave him a dose of opium." My uncle stated, then added "My Lord." He seemed to be growing more afraid. "What about our deal?" He asked trying to sound bolder, but still seeming afraid.

Fire flashed in the eyes of the stranger. Though he was an old man, he seemed to have the vigor of youth in his eyes, even if his hair was gray. "I will take the boy," said the man coldly. For a moment, my uncle seemed to relax. He looked at the man. Their eyes met. I then saw the man's eyes change, they grew more bestial in seconds, in the blink of an eye. His arms came up, stretching out across the fire, at the same time hair seemed to be growing on them at an astonishing speed. I saw him leap across the fire, changing from man into wolf, or some horrid thing in between both forms, I could not tell. I heard my uncle screaming, he ran into the darkness with that shape of hairy man chasing him. I heard more screaming, the screams of a man who knows that his life is over, and he can see death coming, as I can see my own death coming now as I write these words. I will not die as he did though, like a coward. I felt the fear again, it seemed to roll over me like a wave, that brought with it, blackness, and I was falling into that blackness, and then, I knew nothing.

VALENTIUS

I know not how long I slept. I woke up lying in a pile of leaves with dirt in my hair. I did not know where I was or how I had come to be there. I looked around myself and felt incredibly sad and alone. The forest was all around me. The sounds of the birds in the distance were all I could hear. At least the leaves were dry, and I was not that dirty.

I stood up suddenly and thought about my uncle. Where was he? I remembered the dream. It seemed far away now, and the feeling of being alone in that place terrified me. Presently I heard someone walking through the forest toward me and spied the man who had been at the campfire the previous night. He was dressed like a king or a duke, with the finest clothes I had ever seen, and a large, ornate sword hanging from his waist. He smiled at me. I stood still not knowing what to do. We stood there for a moment, and time seemed to slow. Presently I said "Sir, I am lost." He seemed to find this very funny and laughed. I stood there for a moment. "Can you help me find my uncle?" I asked. I need to go home. My mother is probably looking for me.

"You will see your mother again someday." The man stated. "My name is Valentius, and I am your master now." "I am your father, and your mother, and your brother, and all the family you will ever need, and I am going to show you a marvelous secret, a wonderful power." "I am going to make you a werewolf."
At that moment I had an attack of fear. I tried to think of how to run away, but I did not know where I was, or where to run to, and I knew I could not outrun this man, and besides, he was carrying a sword with which he could cut me down. My eyes glanced at the sword and then I looked away. He could obviously see my fear and tell my thoughts. "I killed your uncle." He said simply, "and I will kill you if you try to run away." "There is nowhere that you could run to that I could not find you."

I knew that I was helpless then. "What do you want from me?" I asked, trying to be brave. "I am a wealthy man and a Judge" he said. "You will act as though you are my son, and I will bring you to live with me." "In time I will teach you the method of transformation, and all of the joys and pleasures it brings." "You will be as my son, in this gift of power, and I will give all that I have to you, both my wealth and position, and my power." As he said the word power, there was a tone in his voice that seemed to be as that of a beast, deep, and wild. His eyes grew black, then changed back to blue. "See, it is with me, even in my old age" he said, and I will live longer than ordinary men, and so will you, once I give you the power."

I thought for a moment. My uncle was not a kind man, and he had never treated me with any kind of grace or taught me anything. He had brought me to Valentius thinking that Valentius would eat me, perhaps in exchange for the gift of becoming a werewolf, but instead, Valentius had taken me as his son, and killed my uncle. I did not know what to think of all these things. I remembered the dream, and the screams of my uncle as he died in the darkness outside the light of the campfire. I looked at Valentius. He smiled; his blue eyes seemed kind. What choice did I have? I thought about running away but I knew he would find me. What choice did I have? I had to become a werewolf. The legends were true. They did exist, and I was taken into their world against my will.

"What must I do?" I asked. Valentius seemed pleased I had accepted his offer. I shuddered to think of what might have happened had I not done so. "You will wait here for me, in the forest for a few days while I make arrangements at my house." "I will say that I have adopted a boy from an orphanage, and then bring you into my household." "I need a few days to prepare certain matters." "I will purchase clothes for you, and when you are in my house, you will dress and act with a nature befitting your societal position. We are not beggars," he added sternly.

I looked around me. "Am I to wait here in the woods for you to return?" I asked." "Alone?" I will be sending a servant to help you set up a campsite for the next few days, have no fear" stated Valentius. "I won't let the wolves get you," he said, and then grinned. I wanted to laugh as well, but the whole uncertainty of the situation was too much. I managed a smile, as Valentius walked away. "Stay here" he said over his shoulder, "my servant will come. If you get thirsty, there is a small stream a few dozen yards behind you." Then he was gone. He had not even asked my name.

THE NIGHT COMES-PIERRE

I wandered around until I found the stream and drank deeply. I was very hungry but there was no food. I dared not venture far from the place where I was, as Valentius had warned me to stay there, so that his servant could find me. The day passed slowly. There was no sign of the servant. I grew frightened as the night came closer. Where would I sleep? I looked around for a good pile of leaves and decided that I would try to sleep there if I had to.

I had no way to start a fire, and no food. At least I was not thirsty. Surely the servant would arrive at any moment. Finally, the sun went down, and the night came. I was alone in darkness. The moon was still mostly full, so the night was brightly illuminated. A cool breeze blew through the forest, but I was not cold. I waited to fall asleep, at this time not too afraid, after all that I had seen up until then. Finally, I fell asleep.

At some point in the night, I woke up. I opened my eyes and looked around me. I was not tired anymore and could not sleep so I simply stared into the darkness. I then heard the voice of a child say, "What is your name?" It seemed to come from behind me in the darkness. It was as if some dam of emotion broke inside of me, and I screamed. I screamed and could not stop screaming. Then suddenly I stopped. The woods were quiet. There was only the sound of a few bugs crawling around.

I looked around me. In the moonlight, I could see very well, the trees, the leaves on the forest floor, and the stars up above me. Nothing else. What was I so afraid of anyway? A child? Yet, how could a child be out here in the woods at night? Was it all in my mind? Was I dreaming? I could feel my heart beating and decided that I was not dreaming because I was still breathing hard from all my screaming. Then I decided maybe I was dreaming, and that I was only dreaming that my heart was beating, and my breath was coming in short gasps. Then I decided that it was only a dream so why be afraid, I could not die in a dream, and if I did, I would then wake up. Wouldn't I?

The wind blew, the moon shone, the forest was quiet. The moonlight was very bright. I felt I could see if anything were coming to get me, and I felt fine, "I am still alive" I told myself. Then, "what's your name?" said the child's voice again. This time it came from up above me, in the trees. I could not breathe. The fear was so intense, it simply pulled the wind out of my lungs. It was not that the voice itself scared me, after all, it was only that of a child. It sounded to me almost like that of a baby who has just learned to talk. But the fact that it had come from up in the trees above me terrified me.

I found myself taking in deep gulps of air, my hands thrown out to the sides, and my eyes wide, staring into the darkness. "It is only a child, I tried to tell myself, but how is it up in the trees?" I tried to think of some way that a child could be out here in the woods, in this unknown place. I had no idea where I was. Then the thought occurred to me that this might somehow be the servant promised by Valentius. I gathered up my courage and bravely said "Hello?"

"What is your name?" said the voice, this seeming to come from somewhere behind me. "It's only a child." I told myself. "My name is Peter, Peter Stump." I said bravely, hoping to draw the child out from hiding. Once again, the voice seemed to come from somewhere up in the trees. "Father says I am supposed to look out for you, for a few days, but I don't know why I am supposed to care!" The voice suddenly rose in volume at the last until it was very loud. There seemed to be a boiling rage inside of it. Yet, it was that of maybe a 5- year-old. I pictured an enraged child, somewhere in the treetops.

Silence. The sound of the wind. Moonlight shining upon the leaves. I tried to think of something to say. "How long am I going to be out here?" It seemed to be the most pressing question on my mind. Getting out of the forest, although to where, I could scarcely imagine. Suddenly I decided to be bold, after all, I thought, the child was supposed to be helping me, and sent by Valentius. "Come down here and talk to me, whoever you are," I said. "Maybe I don't want to" the child answered. I could tell where the voice was coming from at least now. A tree directly in front of me, and about 15 feet in the air.

I looked up and could see what appeared to be a naked boy standing on a tree branch in the moonlight. He was about half as tall as me and could not have been 5 years old at most. He was standing on a branch, up in the tree, without holding on to anything else. I would not have dared to stand in such a manner for fear of falling out of the tree. I decided that the boy must have some supernatural power given to him by his father, Valentius.

"Valentius is your father?" I asked. "Adopted" the boy
said. "You are gonna be adopted too, that's why father
says I can't eat you!" His voice had a way of going from
calm, almost bored, to being on the verge of rage at the
very end of a sentence. I felt uneasy and wondered what
the boy might do if angered. "Are there any others of
us.... adopted?" I asked. Then "How big is our family?"
"Who else is in the family?" "Well, we have a sister," said
the child, his tone softening a little bit, "she lives in the
house, I don't live in the house, because Father says I am
too wild, and people would know that I am a wolf, cuz, I
can't be good. I am too wild." He seemed both sad and
frustrated about it, and defiant. "You wanna come down
from that tree, uh, so maybe we can talk?" I asked nicely,
in what I thought was a nice tone of voice. "I am going to
come down from this tree and eat you!" At the last words,
the child was screaming. His voice took on a wolf like
growl with a deep tone to it. I saw his body began to
move in a blur across the tree branch he was standing on.
He was growing hair at a tremendous rate. He fell on all
fours and ran along the branch, and then came running
straight down the trunk of the tree in an impossible and
unnatural way, as if by a twist of nature, gravity had
shifted and was coming from the tree itself.

I fell on my back, and then crawled away in horror with the hot breath of the child werewolf upon my back. I had the fortune to be able to crawl a few steps, and then fell down an embankment into the nearby stream. It was not that deep, but I still sank beneath the water and then came up gasping for air, shaking the water off me and desperately trying to determine my surroundings. The child was nowhere to be seen. I splashed myself out of the river and looked around. I supposed that he had only wanted to scare me and guessed that, child or not, this creature could easily kill me.

It then became clear why our father felt free to let the boy wander in the woods alone at night. I decided then and there not to be afraid anymore, or at least to try not to be afraid. That was hard. So much unknown was in my future. I had no idea when Valentius would return for me, and here I was alone in the woods with an angry wolf child who wanted to eat me but said he had promised not to. The child was a monster, a fiend, out of control as if he had never been spanked and was spoiled. Where was he? Was he coming back? I sank to the ground in exhaustion and stared at the sky. Finally falling asleep again. I seemed to wake a few times or dreamed that a baby wolf was prowling around in the moonlight near me.

KATHERINE

The next morning when I awoke, I was positively starving. With no food, and nothing in the forest to eat, my prospects were grim. I walked in large circles around the spot where I was, and the little stream, but all around me seemed to be nothing but forest, and I dared not venture too far from the spot, or else Valentius might think I had run away, come looking for me and kill me. Finally, I simply returned to the spot where I had been and waited. The day passed slowly, and then became night, and then day again. I saw no sign of the child who had spoken to me on the first night. As the sun was getting close to setting, I saw a girl of what I guessed to be about 14 years of age approaching. I saw no reason to fear her. So, I waited for her to approach. As she got nearer to me, I saw that she had brown hair that hung down to her waist, and that she was wearing a long white dress, with tiny blue flowers embroidered into the seams of it. Among her hair had been braided a few small braids. She seemed altogether lovely and sweet, and I was immediately taken by her.

She came up to me and regarded me calmly with her brown eyes. "My father asked me to bring you this," she said, taking a leather pouch which hung by a sling from her shoulder. She set the bag in between herself and me and stepped back waiting to see my reaction. My hunger overcame my hesitancy, and I opened the pouch, overjoyed to find bread, cheese, and dried meat.

Without asking I tore into the food. She watched me for a while and then said. "What is your name little boy?" I did not feel little, after all that I had endured in the past few days and lifted my shoulders slightly to show her as much. "Peter" I said between bites of bread and cheese. "Who are you?" "My name is Katherine." She said calmly. I felt that she was being kind to me in her tone, and I was very appreciative of any gentle words, after the fright I had experienced in the past several days. Seeing this girl act civilized toward me, and bring food lifted my spirits greatly. "Is Valentius your father as well?" I asked. "Yes" she answered, "adopted." I took advantage of her willingness to talk and asked her more questions. "How many of us are there?" meaning how many adopted children. "There are three of us children, 5 in the family" she said. "Myself, you, Pierre, Father, and Grandmother."

"Have you met Pierre?" she asked. I thought of the boy in the trees and said that I had met a boy in the darkness who had threatened to eat me. She smiled and said that that was indeed Pierre. "Father spoils him" she said. "He wants him to live in the house, but Pierre is too wild and won't obey Father, so Father makes him live out here." She gestured to the forest around us. A few birds chirped in the treetops. She looked at me as if wondering if I could behave or was going to be an uncivilized monster like Pierre for a brother. I looked back at her calmly and she seemed to be satisfied that I had at least some manners. She looked off in the distance then, as the sun had begun to set, and the shadows were growing longer.

"I must be going now, as father says I must be home before dark." I wondered if her home was far, and if I would soon be living there. "What about me?" I asked anxiously, wishing to be out of the forest. "Oh, you will be all right," she said, smiling gently. Father says you can't come to the house just yet, he is still making arrangements to find the right witch to adopt you from." She stressed the word adopt carefully. "But it will be soon I am sure, not more than a few weeks" she added kindly as if trying to console.

I did not know what she meant about my adoption, but she had to go so I decided to put on a brave face and show her that I was not scared. She seemed to guess that I did not want to stay in the forest alone, and her tone was soft as she said "Don't worry about a thing, Pierre is out here, and he won't disobey Father and eat you, he wouldn't dare, and he will see to it that no one or no creature bother you, believe me, he will be looking after you, he is never far from you, even though you may not hear him, or see him." She looked around us into the empty forest and said loudly "Isn't that right little Pierre?" as if he were somewhere close and could hear her. Then she winked at me, turned on her heels, and walked into the forest.

The night came. I clutched the leather purse Katherine had given me close and decided to try to ration the bread, cheese, and meat for a few days. I sat with my back against a tree and fell asleep peacefully. I awoke several times during the night to the sounds of howling wolves in the distance, but I had nowhere to run to, so I just sat there until I fell asleep again. At times I would wake up and see wolves walking through the shadows of the moonlight in the distance. I dared not breathe then, but only sat in silence.

Three days passed, and Katherine returned. She asked if I had seen Pierre, and I said that I had not, but that at night, I sometimes saw wolves in the distance. She did not seem particularly concerned by this and asked if I would like to see "the house." I guessed that this was the place where I would be staying and said I would very much like to. She said that we would walk for some distance, until we had reached "the back yard" and could see the house from there. She then led me some distance into the woods where eventually we came to a large pond surrounded by trees.

In the center of the pond was a small Island. On the island was a small castle. It consisted of a house of four stories height, entirely made of stone, with a tower at the back side of the house that seemed to be impossibly tall. I thought it was the type of house that a duke or perhaps the brother of a king might live in. I had never seen such a place up close, only in the pages of storybooks. The waters of the pond were calm and still. A few frogs jumped after bugs here and there. The sun shone bright above us, and the whole scene was very calming. I began to like Valentius very much and think that perhaps he was a man of great importance. I wondered why he had chosen to adopt me. After all, it was only a small family of three children. Why me? Was it only because my uncle had brought me to him as a sacrifice? Had he planned to eat me and then changed his mind at the last moment?

Katherine sat calmly down on a fallen log. She looked over at the house and so did I. All was quiet. I tried to picture myself living there, and what life would be like when it happened. What would I do? I suddenly realized I was dressed in filthy clothes and covered in dirt. Katherine on the other had was shining, clean, and dressed in white clothes. I thought she must be an angel she looked so sweet to me. She seemed to notice how dirty I was then, as if she could tell what I was thinking and said, "we will get you fresh clothes and a bath when you are brought into the house, you know." It was just a statement. I smiled and nodded, and things were comfortable between us. She had a way of putting me at ease almost like a mother. The way she spoke to me was like a mother or an older sister would, as if she was trying to explain things to me, about my new family, the things I needed to know.

She seemed to be in no hurry to leave, and so I took the opportunity to ask her more questions. First, about herself. "When did you get adopted?" I asked. ""Did you have a life before this?" "I don't remember one." she said. "Father found me and Grandmother in a cave, I was only a baby then."" And Grandmother does not speak, so I don't really know where I come from." I tried to process this information. "Oh" I said, not knowing what to say next. "What about Pierre? How did he get adopted?"

She paused for a moment and thought, as if considering how to explain things to me. "Well, his father was a werewolf, and, our Father killed him, and took the baby, when Pierre was three years old. So, Pierre had already begun to develop. He could hunt and kill for himself when Father took him. Father did not really even need to adopt him, Pierre could have easily lived on his own in the woods even at that age.... He.....is a killer...." She said trailing off at the end. "Anyway, I suppose I must take you back to the forest now, I am sure you will be brought into the house soon, you seem like a nice young man to me." I found myself smiling that she had called me a young man rather than a boy. She led me back to the forest, to the place where I had been, and then left me there again.

THE CAPTURE OF PIERRE

The next three days and nights passed without anything happening. On the third night I woke up to the sounds of voices. Dozens of men were coming in my direction through the forest. I could hear their loud and excited voices, and they carried torches which illuminated their faces. By this time the moon was not so full, and the night was dark. I few clouds wandered about in the sky sometimes cutting off what light there was. For the first time, I became very aware of the cycles of the moon, and how it provided all light that existed in the night, in the woods.

I wanted to run but did not want to get lost. Soon the men would be on my position. I looked up; the tree I had been accustomed to sleep against had a few low-lying branches. I reached for one and pulled myself into the tree. I climbed up into the tree a little way, and saw the men pass below me, and off into the night, as they did so, I could hear a little bit of their conversation, drifting on the wind. "They say the monster is the size of a child..."and then another voice "...must catch it alive..." I realized they had hunting dogs with them and were following a trail. The dogs led them off to the side of my campsite, and then in a large circle around the area where I was.

I could hear the barking of the dogs and see the light of the torches in the distance as they went in a complete circle around me, hundreds of yards wide. The thought occurred to me that the monster they were hunting was Pierre, and that he had probably paced the perimeter of my location many times. After the second time around the men stopped, and the dogs begin to get excited. I heard screaming, and what sounded to be a fight. What if they had tracked Pierre to that tree, where he was watching me, protecting me, even though he did not, for some reason, wish to speak with me or be friendly? I strained my neck to look and see what was happening in the distance.

More screams, I knew that someone had just died horribly from the sound of it. Men only scream like that when they are having their gut ripped out by swords, or claws and teeth. I wanted to get closer. I wondered if I was in danger. If the men had somehow found Pierre, he was certainly not going to hurt me. Part of me knew I should stay where I was, safe. The other part did not care. In moments I was down from the tree and running toward the sounds of the fighting and the glow of the torchlight.

As I grew closer, I could see that the men had driven stakes into the ground around the tree in a large circle. The stakes were long, and lit like torches at the top, so that the entire area around the tree was lit up. This in combination with the half moon, lit up the scene to the brightness of almost daylight. As I got closer, I could see the bodies of several men lying on the trampled ground. Their throats were slashed, and in one case, the man had completely lost his head. Four other men lay on the ground moaning with various types of wounding. I saw Pierre, eyes mad with rage, leap over a body, and latch on to another one of the men with both hands, feet, and teeth. His form was somewhere between man and wolf. He was covered with hair, and his little body moved with viscous speed. I saw him rip that man apart in moments. The blood flying everywhere, the awful screams piercing the night.

Another man on the edge of the scene let loose three large dogs, they ran at Pierre, and all latched on to him at once. He fought them all at once, and for a moment all that could be seen was a blur of fur and teeth. Then Pierre stood still, he grabbed the first dog with both hands and ripped out its throat with both teeth. At that time both other dogs were hanging on to him with their jaws clenched, shaking, and writhing all over the place. When the first dog was dead Pierre pulled the second one off and ripped it apart as well. The third dog let go and ran away in fear with its tail between its legs.

Covered in blood, Pierre turned his attention on the remaining four men. Two of them had pitchforks raised in defense, and the other two had raised a net between them and were spreading it apart at about ten feet. The two men with the pitchforks ran to stand behind the net. I wondered at this curious strategy. Pierre raised his hands and took a few steps forward. He stumbled drunkenly and then fell to his knees. He must be hurt, I thought to myself. The men did not hesitate for even a moment, they ran toward Pierre, engulfing his little body in the net, knocking him down. The men who had been waiting behind the net ran forward screaming "get him" or something to that effect. The slammed their pitchforks into the body of Pierre, pinning him to the ground. "Tie him!" They screamed "we have not long!"

The men who had been holding the net drew ropes from their pockets and tied Pierre in all sorts of ways. They jumped and screamed and howled and congratulated each other on their catch. I took the opportunity to slink back into the forest out of the range of the torchlight. I climbed a tree and watched to see what would happen next. The men begin to move quickly. They pulled up the torches and gathered the dead bodies of the other men together in a pile. I could hear them talking excitedly but could not make out many of the words. "Let's take him to the cave at Bedbur....."""...only a child, are there more of them?" ".....Let's get out of here, my god lets go, let's go" They seemed to be in an incredible hurry. "Should we burn the bodies?"" ....no, take them with us, leave the dogs" At that point they disappeared over a hill, and the voices and the light were gone.

What now? I took stock of my situation. What could I do? I knew that Valentius would want to know about this, what he would do to those men, I could not imagine. Should I go to the house and tell him? It was still early in the night, or so it seemed. I knew that I was not supposed to go to the house, I was supposed to be waiting in the woods for Valentius to make arrangements. Yet I also knew that he considered Pierre his son, and that he would surely want to know if he had been kidnapped. I thought I could find my way to the house and began to run towards it in the dim moonlight. I took me about two hours to reach it.

By this time, it was perhaps midnight, or one in the morning. I saw the house, like a miniature castle, reflected in the moonlight of the pond. It occurred to me that I did not know how to knock on the door, or from which direction the door might be. I prowled around the edges of the pond in the darkness, ordinarily I would have not been so bold, but the circumstances pushed me forward. After I had circled around the whole distance of the pool, I realized that on one side of the house, was a door, with steps leading down from the door into the murky water. On the bank opposite from this, concrete steps led out of the water. It was as if, it was meant for someone to walk down the steps into the water, and then out of the water, up the steps to the door. I paused for a moment considering this, standing on the set of steps that were on the bank of the pond.

The house was quiet, and no lights or candles shone in the windows. Were they asleep? My mind imagined Katherine, Valentius, and "grandmother" somewhere in the house asleep. The thought of going into the water terrified me. I don't know why, I knew how to swim, and could have swam to the steps on the other side of the water. But what unknown horrors lay beneath the water? I shivered to think. Somewhere a frog jumped, or a bug splashed into the water. Silence. What now. Suddenly I found myself screaming. "Hello!" Silence.

A light came on in one window. I thought I heard movement. A window then opened on the second floor. "Peter?" What are you doing here?" It was Katherine. "Pierre has been taken!" "Stolen!" I yelled. "I can't stay in the woods alone with no one to protect me!" I added. My fear and trauma over the past week overcame all thoughts of holding back by this time "Help me!" I pleaded. "I don't even know what's going on anymore!" Suddenly I felt like a child again, on the verge of tears. The window closed. I waited for the front door to open. It was set perhaps ten or eleven steps up from the water, and maybe 30 feet away from the bank of the pond where I was standing.

The door flew open, Valentius was standing there naked. His eyes were wild. "Where have they taken him?" he screamed. His voice boomed over the water, and I shrunk back in fear. ""I don't know" I said timidly. Hair seemed to grow from every part of his body at once as he transformed. He leaped over the pool of water in one swift moment and stood beside me once again in human form. "What did you see?" He asked me quickly. I told him as fast as I could what had happened, and where Pierre had been taken from. As soon as I had described this to him, he became a wolf, not partly man and partly wolf, but full wolf, and ran into the darkness at great speed, simply leaving me standing there.

Katherine appeared in the doorway in a nightgown. "I suppose you can come in," she said. "Father did not say it was ok, but I don't think he would expect you to stay out there, and it is only grandmother and I in the house, so you may come in, if you can cross the water." "How do I cross the water?" I asked. "You must swim" she replied. "It's ok, nothing will get you, the water is safe. Just swim toward me." I hesitated, but I wanted to go to the house. Katherine seemed so nice. Maybe inside the house, I would be safe at last. "Come on, its ok, she said soothingly, you can do it, just swim across to me." I took a step down into the water. I could feel it cover my feet. I could feel the cold stone steps under me, leading onward, toward the house. Katherine stood in the doorway, a light shining behind her. "Cmon" she said again, holding out her hands toward me.

I kept walking, deeper and deeper into the pond. I could still feel the stone steps under my feet, soon the water covered my head, I swam for a few strokes, and then could feel the steps under my feet again, and I walking up the banks toward the door of the house. "There there, you did it, see its ok." Katherine said. I felt like I could trust her, as she led me into the house into a large central room where a few candles were lit. I was cold from the pool and shivering. "Let me make a fire get you warmed up." She spoke. "Sit down here, in front of the fireplace." I sat down as she busied herself making a fire. I felt very tired and sleepy. After the fire was lit, it was very warm, and I wanted to lie on a soft rug before the fire. Katherine went away and returned with a piece of bread and a strip of dried meat for me to eat. I devoured these things, and laid down in front of the fire, watching its dancing flames cast shadows around the room. "You can go to sleep if you want to," said Katherine. She must have noticed the dazed look on my face. I wanted to sleep. "OK" I said, "Ok." Then I was falling into the darkness. And I slept.

GRANDMOTHER

Sometime during the night, I awoke to the sound of footsteps. The fire had died down and I guessed that Katherine had come to add more wood to it. I saw her enter the room in a nightgown and put a few logs on the fire. Then she sat down in a large chair near the fire, facing me. The way she sat in the chair was less ladylike than the way she normally carried herself. Her hair was also strewn about and unkempt. She looked over at me and smiled, a certain playful grin, and then her body begin to grow hair very quickly. In moments she was a wolf, sitting in the chair. The sight was somehow amusing to me.

She leaped out of the chair in wolf form, and ran from the room, only to run back into the room a few moments later. I somehow knew that she wanted me to chase her. I wanted to chase her very much, and as I stood to my feet to do so, I realized that I was growing hair all over my body as well. I fell to the floor and could see that my hands were now transformed into the paws of a wolf. Instinctively, I began to run after Katherine. I ran through the doorway into the next room, and ran headlong into her, our wolf bodies colliding and then bouncing off each other. The next thing I knew, she had ran further into the house and I was running after her.

I chased her from room to room. The house seemed larger than it looked like from the outside. We went up stairways, and down stairways. Through rooms full of clothes, and rooms for cooking, libraries, even a room full of swords and armor. Valentius was not lying when he said, "we are not poor." I ran and ran and did not seem to grow tired. Soon Katherine led me to a spiral stairway. It went up and up and up. I guessed that this might be the tower I had seen from the outside. Candles burned in little niches in the walls, higher and higher we ran. I thought it must be impossible that we could climb so far, that the tower could be this tall. Finally, we burst into a room at what must have been the top of the tower.

The room was perhaps 40 feet across and round. Moonlight shone in from the windows, and a few candles burned in a niche in the wall. In the center of the room, was a huge gray wolf. It looked to be perhaps 3 times the size of the largest wolf ever born. Its fur was very gray, almost white, and it was sleeping. Katherine stopped running and sat on her haunches, still in the form of a wolf. I stopped and stared. I looked at her, she looked at me. I looked at the huge sleeping wolf on the floor. It looked old. Even its face was wrinkled, all the hair around its eyes was completely white, and patchy as if some of it had started to fall out, showing pink skin underneath. Even still, I feared what would happen if it woke up and grew angry. It must have weighed 500 pounds and was nearly the size of a cow. It was sleeping peacefully.

Then the sleeping wolf opened one eye. I stared into that massive black eye for a moment. I was sort of hypnotized by it. It seemed to be impossibly large, and it looked like it was slowly changing color from black to dark blue. Little stars appeared among the blue. It was pulling me into it. The eye was growing larger and larger, or I was growing smaller. Then the blue part of the eye, with the stars in it, became the night sky, and it was the sky I was standing under.

I became aware of a crowd of people around me. They were holding torches and dressed in filthy rags or animal skins. I had the strange feeling that I was inside of a dream and seeing something from a very long time ago. Men and women murmured in low voices. Before the crowd of perhaps 50 people stood a raised platform made of small logs that had been bound together and then raised up by means of poles. The platform was perhaps 5 feet raised in the air. Two poles rose into the air from the surface of the platform. Between the two poles stood a naked woman of perhaps 19 years of age. Her arms were bound at the wrist and stretched out toward each of the poles that stood on either side of her. Two incredibly old women with long gray hair stood on either side of her.

On low tables before them were large clay bowls filled with something I could not see. The crowd murmured quietly in awe. The old women on either side of the tied girl between the poles began to reach into the bowls on the small tables in front of them. They seemed to get a paste from the bowls on their hands, and they began to smear the paste onto the naked body of the tied girl. The paste was white, with light green mixed within it. Bits of what appeared to be leaves were also in the paste and stuck to the body of the girl as the old women rubbed it on her skin from the neck down. She waited calmly not making any sound.

Eventually the old women had applied the white and green paste to most of the girl's body. I wondered at the meaning of all this strange ritual, and the fact that I had changed back to human form. I stood among the people who were watching the ritual, but none of them seemed to notice me. At this time, the older women placed a large wolf skin around the girl, completely wrapping her body with the skin. The girl made a sound like "uuuuuuuuuuh" that seemed to be part pleasure, part pain. Her eyes rolled back in her head, and she swayed as if drunk. If she had not been tied to the poles, one arm tied to each, she would have fallen to the ground.

At that moment, the crowd parted, and a man came forward carrying a baby sheep in his arms. He approached the raised platform, and by a series of steps on the side, climbed up to the top of it. The girl tied between the poles did not seem to notice him. She hung somewhat limply from the poles she was tied to, covered in the whitish green paste, and the wolf-skin tied around her. The claws of the wolf were still intact on the skin and draped over her chest. The tail of the wolf was also intact and hung down to touch the floor of the platform. The man holding the little lamb walked in front of the girl and held it up in front of her face. She jerked suddenly, her whole body twitched for a moment and became rigid, then swayed again. Her eyes rolled around wildly, somewhere between conscious and unconscious.

The people around me began slowly chanting some unknown language. I could not understand what they were saying, but it felt like they were calling on a god or praying. The man on the platform waved the lamb in front of the tied girl again. She jerked and twitched wildly now, as if she could not control her limbs. The crowd increased the intensity of its chanting as if drawing toward a climax. Suddenly the man drew a long knife from somewhere and quickly slit the throat of the lamb. He held it towards the tied girl and its blood spurted out toward her, with drops of it splashing on her face. He let forth a mighty yell and held the dead lamb high in the air with one hand, its blood dripping down its arm. He shook it in front of the face of the tied girl.

It was then that her eyes changed. She lunged forward as if to bite the lamb with her mouth. The man took a step back and held it away from her. She screamed incoherently, a beastly inhuman sound and strained against the leather bonds tying her wrists to the poles. The crowd stopped chanting and watched intently. The old women on the stage raised their hands and signaled for the crowd to keep chanting. At that moment lightning flashed across the sky illuminating the scene as bright as daylight.

The man on the stage then threw the lamb into the air, and the woman, eyes wild, broke free from her bonds with a snarl, leaping forward to bite the lamb, and in doing so, her human form fell away, and she became a wolf. The woman was gone. She leaped from the platform. With the lamb in her mouth, fully a wolf at this time. The crowd drew back, and the chanting became a hushed awe, they formed a ring around the wolf, and I could not see what was happening. I fell down, and stood back up, and then for a moment I saw the stars above me, and knew I was dreaming, and then I was falling into darkness.

VALENTIUS RETURNS

In the morning, I woke up sitting in the chair by the fire. I don't know how I got there. Perhaps I had been chilled, for I was wrapped in a large wolfskin. I don't know if Katherine had given it to me at some point or not, but it would seem so. I thought I had remembered falling asleep by the fire, under a blanket. A few coals still lingered, so I got up and added some logs. The blaze soon took the chill off the room. I dared not wander in the house, because I was new there, and still felt like a stranger. Katherine was nowhere to be seen. After some time, I began to grow bored and wonder what was in the other rooms of the house. I thought I had seen them in the dream I had during the night and wanted to see if they looked anything like the dream.

The house was quiet, but the sun was up, surely it would not hurt for me to wander around a bit and look at things? I walked to a large window opposite of the fireplace and looked out. A low mist hung over the pond. Clouds hung low in the morning sky, and it looked as if it might rain. I looked around the room. It was bare except for a few chairs and the fireplace. At the far end of the room was an archway leading to another room. I hesitated for a moment and then walked towards the doorway.

It was my house. I had been invited to live there. I decided to see what the rest of the house looked like. I walked into the next room; it was full of weapons. Swords, armor, spears, crossbows, and ball and chain mace type weapons hung on the walls. Some were new, without scratches, and others looked to have been used in battle at some time. Beyond this was another room with many large windows. It was full of potted plants, some with long, trumpet shaped flowers of white, and some with purple. Some sort of vine plant climbed a trellis in front of the window. I walked over and stood next to the window. The fog over the pond had lifted, but, the rainclouds still moved about in the sky angrily.

I bent to examine one of the flowers and try to smell it. "Be careful with that Stramonium" a voice said behind me, "it's a deadly poison you know, and it can drive men to madness, to believe that they have become wolves, or many other such creatures." It was Valentius. I hoped I had not done wrong by wandering the house. "Did you find Pierre?" I asked. Valentius seemed calm and was dressed royally again. He carried no sword with him. "Let us talk" Valentius said. He seemed as if he had much to say but was in no hurry to say it.

He signaled me to follow him into another room, this one a library. The room was not large, perhaps only 10 by 20 feet in size. Several large bookshelves occupied the corners and there were perhaps 200 books on them. Valentius sat down on in a chair and indicated that I was to sit in another chair. He opened a window, so that some light could shine in, and then sat down across from me. "I did not find Pierre" he began, "but I found someone who knows where he is." He sighed, then said "It is time I explain some things to you, about who you are, and who I am and how I came to be what I am." He looked at me as if measuring my ability to grasp the things that he was about to tell me. "There are two types of werewolves, some who are born, and some who are made. "" You, me, Katherine, Grandmother, we are, or, well, you will be, a made werewolf."

"Pierre was...is, not like us, he was born being what he is." "I....I was not born this way" he said. "I learned of the method of transformation, along with another man, through the study of a rare book." "We discovered a method from combining the instructions in the legends and lore of the werewolf. We perfected that method together. Nicholas still lives, he is a dangerous man, almost purely instinct by now..."" dangerous" he said again. I guessed that Nicholas had been a friend of his once, but perhaps they had had a falling out. He did not elaborate.

"The born wolves are werewolves that come by it naturally, for some reason they were born with the ability to do it." "They are, not nearly as strong as made wolves, and they do not live as long. They are mostly a foul race of criminals, thieves, and murderers, which I slay when I come across, but I will never be able to eradicate them fully from the Earth, because more are born every generation. Fortunately, only perhaps one in 20,000 people is a born wolf, so there are not that many of them. Most of them around this area live in a cave just outside of the city of Bedbur."

I remembered the men who captured Pierre saying that they wanted to "take him to the cave at Bedbur" and asked Valentius about it. "Were those men werewolves who captured Pierre?" I asked. "No, he answered, but they work for the group of werewolves at Bedbur, the born wolves." Then he added "Pierre is not coming back, he is with them now, and I am sure that they will have told him, what he is." "I don't know where they have hidden him, and I dare not enter the cave to look for him, I am afraid that they will have turned him to their point of view."

He paused and looked at me. "What is their point of view?" I asked. "That humans are food." He answered simply. He looked at me as if judging my reaction. I thought about how savage Pierre had been and wondered if the other born wolves were like him. "The born wolves are more savage than we are, they have no morality, they use their ability to transform, for criminal acts of cruelty. They simply take what they want from society and use the gift they possess for evil." "We on the other hand, are students of nature, mystics, sorcerers." "Are there any others like us?" I asked. "Well, there is Nicholas," he answered. "And I believe he has a student, but I have never met the student. Nicholas hides him or her from me, I don't know why, and I don't know of any others, If they exist or not.

The transformation that Nicholas and I discovered...It was only known by a few, and I do not know who wrote the books that we learned from." He paused and looked intently into space, then added "I am sure, that, somewhere out there, there are more, but those are all I know of." "Of the born wolves, I know of perhaps 30 in the region. As I have said, they live mostly in the cave at Bedbur." I struggled to grasp all this information and place it within my worldview. "Do they know about us?" I asked. "Yes, he answered, and they fear us. They do not know what gives us our power, it is a secret. They do not know how I was transformed, or the method of making a made wolf." I wanted to know the method, and yet dared not ask, since he had said, it was a secret. I squirmed in my chair. Valentius seemed to guess what I was thinking.

"You have much to learn to become a part of our family" he said. "First, Katherine will teach you how to read, and then I will teach you how to use weapons and fight." "I am sure that you will kill many werewolves and witches in your day, if you survive, and can accomplish the transformation." You may live as long as 300 years!" He said that with an awe in his voice. Then he looked at me and plainly said "I am 200 years old." I found this fascinating. Valentius appeared to be only perhaps 50, and was still filled with a vigor, and a fire in his eyes. He was both comforting and frightening to me. I wanted to know his secrets, and though he had told me much, I thought I could learn so much more from him. "How do I do it?" I asked. "How do I transform?" He looked at me and smiled. "It has already begun" he said.

He stood up, "I must leave now" he said. "I have business to attend to. Katherine will watch over you and begin your studies. You may go into any room in the house except the tower that is only for Grandmother." "Katherine will begin your education; I will return in a few days. There is plenty of food in the pantry. You and Katherine are not to leave the house while I am gone. You are safe here." He smiled again, and then added "I won't let the wolves get you," as if it was some sort of private joke for him, or he was dwelling on some memory from long ago. Then he walked from the room leaving me sitting in the library.

I thought for a moment and considered my situation. It seemed that for the time, I had it good. I had gone from rags to riches. From a family of weak, dirty criminals including my uncle who had tried to feed me to Valentius, to having a new family of powerful, wealthy people who had incredible knowledge to teach me. The house seemed warm, comfortable, majestic, like something out of a fairy tale. Surrounded by a moat and built like a castle, it also seemed very safe. I sat quietly thinking about all that was to come, and what kind of a life I wanted to lead. Then...

Explanation of the Text by the Author:

Hello, my name is Arundell Overman, and I would like to tell you a little of how the previous two stories came to be written by me, and the hidden meaning behind them. I suppose I should start at the beginning....

Many years ago, a friend brought a book to my house. It was called "The Werewolf in Lore and Legend" and was written by a strange Catholic Priest named Montague Summers. Montague completely believed in werewolves and his book gives lots of blood-soaked tales of the old werewolves such as Peter Stubbe. My friend gave me the book as a present, he proudly announced that he had stolen it from a local library and that "something" told him to give it to me. Looking back, I am sure that some spirit directed him to bring me the book.

As a man who has spent my whole life in the study of the occult, of course I was interested in studying werewolves. I was amazed by how much lore and legends there were and reading about the old werewolf trials. At some point I distinctly felt something watching me read the book. I did not want to admit it to myself, but I knew that it was the spirit of a werewolf.

I was fascinated by the power and energy in the book. Most of the werewolves were probably crazed killers, and not really werewolves at all, but I noticed after a lot of research, that the phenomenon was somewhat different than might be expected. There were some common themes that ran through the old legends. First, Werewolves were not made through being bitten by other werewolves, that is an idea developed in Hollywood, and based off the vampire, because Hollywood did not really know how werewolves were made. The truth is that in the old legends, in most cases, werewolves were witches who used a magic oil made from the fat of an animal, mixed with various herbs which produced effects like LSD or Magic Mushrooms.

From what I can tell, there were at least people TRYING to become werewolves in the old days. Maybe they just got high on drugs and ran around in the forest with a wolfskin tied to them and THOUGHT they became werewolves because they were tripping so hard. Perhaps that truly does account for some of the phenomena. Certainly, some of those people who were accused of such crimes as being a witch or a werewolf were innocent, or even mentally ill. Yet, I am convinced that there are real witches, and there are real werewolves.

I almost did not write this book. Valentius twisted my arm the whole way. What? The reason I say this is, I believe Valentius is real. He lived a real life sometime back there in history. Maybe I did not get every detail correct, but many of the scenes in the book, that stuff really happened. I can't tell you what parts of it are real and what parts are not. All I know is that a spirit named Valentius appeared to me and gave me the story. He was once a real man who lived and was an alchemist, and he practiced out of the old grimoires such as the Book of Abramelin, Keys of Solomon, and other such books.

I am not asking you to believe me, I am not trying to start a religion. I am only stating the facts as I know them. For more information on Werewolves, see my book "The Werewolf in Theory and Practice," and my other book "The Grimoire of Valentius the Werewolf. There is much more to this whole story and my involvement in it found in those works, and real rituals for becoming a werewolf for those bold or foolish enough to carry out such things.

A few notes on the two stories presented here that may be of interest to the reader. The stories take place over a hundred years apart. In the first story, written by Valentius himself, he is a young man of around 20, and this is the time when he becomes a werewolf. The second story is written around 180 years later by Peter Stubbe, and at that time Valentius is an old man, and a master werewolf with great powers.

I only wrote the stories as they were given to me, and I can add nothing to them or take anything away from them, because they present a kind of mythology, the mythology of a powerful spirit I know as Valentius. A few details that I know as the writer are that Nicholas became Nicholas Remy, a notorious witch hunter who sent 900 men and women to their deaths. He became cruel over the years and was the opposite of Valentius who became kind and philosophical, a man of reason, culture, science, and music. He could play several instruments and composed music that was connected to spiritual forces in some way, when you heard it, you were transported to other dimensions, in the case of his music, you were allowed to see into a parallel dimension where Marcus lived. This idea is like the old legends of humans being taken to fairy land. Marcus, and now Valentius live in that other dimension, where they do not age, or perhaps age slowly.

The Queen is never spoken of by her name in the story, and I am not sure what it was. I call her the Painted lady, because in the times I have seen her, she had on a lot of makeup. To put it simply, she looked like a 17th century prostitute in both her dress and subtle characteristics. I also call her Valentia, but I think her name is Maria, and her full name is Maria Valentia. She truly scares me. I don't know if the Peter Stubbe in the story is connected to the historical Peter Stubbe, but its possible, in the end, Nicholas Remy got him, and he was burned at the stake as a werewolf. And I don't mean the Historical Nicholas Remy. For me using these names was only symbolic of the fates of these characters. Nicholas became evil, cruel, and Peter was captured by the Inquisition, of which Nicholas eventually was a key player in.

And now we come to the end of my work. I don't have all the answers to what these creatures are. But I am satisfied that I have fulfilled my pact in writing about them to the very best of my ability in return for the spiritual gifts they have given me. With these words I wish you peace profound, and the best of luck on your path.

-Arundell Overman

Back CVR: This is the story of Valentius, a 17th century alchemist who discovered the secret of how to become a werewolf through experimenting with a book which was taken from witches who were burned at the stake. Through the creation of a special oil to be rubbed on the skin, the wearing of a wolfskin, and conjuring 7 ghosts and 5 demons, he gained the power. He became a man of great wisdom yet saw the tragic results of the werewolf transformation in his friend Nicholas, and his lover, the Queen of France. This story is a form of mythology for witches and magicians and is intended to transmit an understanding of the personality of a very real spirit, the ghost of a werewolf named Valentius.

Notes: